THE
BONEMENDER'S OATH

HOLLY BENNETT

ORCA BOOK PUBLISHERS

Library and Archives Canada Cataloguing in Publication

Bennett, Holly, 1957-

The bonemender's oath / Holly Bennett.

ISBN 1-55143-443-1

I. Title.
PS8603.E5595B66 2006   jC813'.6   C2006-902526-6

Summary: In this sequel to *The Bonemender*, Gabrielle and her brother Tristan
fight to keep safe those they care for and to find a place for love in their lives.

First published in the United States 2006
Library of Congress Control Number: 2006926564

Orca Book Publishers gratefully acknowledges the support for its publishing programs provided by the following agencies: the Government of
Canada through the Book Publishing Industry Development Program and
the Canada Council for the Arts, and the Province of British Columbia
through the BC Arts Council and the Book Publishing Tax Credit.

Cover artwork, cover design, interior map: Cathy Maclean
Typesetting: Christine Toller

In Canada:
PO Box 5626, Stn. B
Victoria, BC   Canada
V8R 6S4

In the United States:
PO Box 468
Custer, WA USA
98240-0468

www.orcabook.com
Printed and bound in Canada.

09 08 07 06 • 5 4 3 2 1

Printed on 100% old growth forest free paper that is 50% post
consumer waste, 100% recycled and chlorine free.

UNKNOWN TERRITORY: GREFFIER

KRYLIAN MOUNTAINS

SKYWAY PASS

SMOKY RIVER

EASTERN GATEWAY

LOUTRE

STONE WATER

OTTER LAKE

WESTERN PASS

GAUDETTE

TURLEAU

LA MARONNE

GAMIER

BATÎME

RATIGOUCHE

MIRAMET

AVINE RIVER

PICKEREL RIVER

BARILLES

VERDEAU

CHÊNIER

RIVARD

HOOK POINT

BLANCHETTE

BARILLES CLIFFS

CROW ISLAND

GRAY SEA

THE KRYLIAN BASIN

LOWLAND CLEARED, FARMLAND
UPLAND PASTURE
WOODLAND

BORDER
TOWN
PASS
BRIDGE OR FORD
ROAD

This one's for my dad. We miss you.

ACKNOWLEDGMENTS:

Authors do not squeeze writing into their "spare time" without their families feeling it, so I want to thank my husband John and three wonderful sons for their enthusiasm and support, even when I spend the entire weekend hunkered over the computer or am only half at the dinner table because my other half is wandering around in la-la land. Thanks also to my editor, Maggie de Vries, who makes the hard work of revision *almost* painless and claims to cry at the sad parts of my stories.

CHAPTER ONE

IS father had done it better, Derkh thought. As usual. To be killed all at once, have it done with—that was Col's style. A soldier's death. And Derkh? He would die slowly, without honor, forgotten in a cart at the arse-end of a battlefield.

The surgeons, busy with casualties from the night raid that killed his father, had not thought to check on the wounded boy they had given up on days before. No one had even brought food or water until sunset of the following day. He had asked that man to fetch a surgeon.

"I'll tell 'em," the soldier had promised, but the accompanying shrug suggested, Don't get your hopes up.

The next morning the fever was back—a hot/cold ache in his joints and behind his eyeballs—and a hungry flame licked at his belly. Still no one came. Derkh thought about trying to change the bandaging himself. He even forced himself to sit up despite the knifing pain and dizziness—but he would never manage to strike a fire and brew up the herbs Gabrielle had left him.

By the time a surgeon appeared in his tent, Derkh's thoughts were drifting, unconnected fragments, but he tried to pull them together and relay Gabrielle's instructions.

"There's no time, soldier," the surgeon replied. "We're heading out now."

Derkh hoped Gabrielle had made it out alive. It was the only hope he had left.

"DERKH? ARE YOU all right? Are you in pain?"

Gabrielle's face, rocking back and forth with the motion of the cart, was inches from his. She must have been recaptured, he realized with sorrow. Then his head cleared, and he was in the present again.

"No, I'm fine. Sorry. I was dreaming, I guess."

But was it a dream? Dreams were nonsense; this was memory so vivid it seemed real. Derkh wasn't even sure he had been asleep. He knew he would just as soon forget the things his mind insisted on reliving.

But now he was waking, and it was the present that loomed large. They were nearing Chênier. Gabrielle had conveyed this news cheerfully, as though he should be glad of it. She didn't seem to realize that the end of this long journey south was not a homecoming for him.

Derkh had seen the hard looks from the Verdeau men—not those who served under Gabrielle's brother, Tristan, but others. They wondered, and rightly, why a prisoner of war was cosseted like a long-lost relative. He was a Greffaire soldier and before long would have to answer to that charge. And what then? Prison? Slavery? Execution, after Gabrielle's long labor to save him? The rule of Verdeau and the will of the king's officers would decide; a healer's friendship would not be enough to protect him.

Derkh pushed himself to sitting, ignoring the protest in his belly. He would walk for a while, for as long as Gabrielle would allow, and he would savor each painful step. Whatever his fate, it seemed certain his days of walking free under the summer sun were coming to an end.

TRISTAN HAD TO rein in his horse at the sight of the familiar towers of the castle, gray stone outlined against the perfect blue of an early summer sky. Home. The banners bearing Verdeau's green and white were playful in the breeze.

Only a season it had been since Tristan had headed out with the Verdeau army to meet the invaders from the north. One brutal spring, filled with more horror and loss than he had ever known. He had thought coming home would be the easy part.

But nothing he had faced had been harder than this: riding into his own courtyard a day ahead of the returning army, so that his mother would not have to hear from a messenger that her husband, King Jerome DesChênes of Verdeau, would not be coming home at all.

The road approaching Chênier was studded with sentries, Tristan noted with approval. No doubt his brother Dominic had undertaken the defense of the city with his usual competence.

Then it was his own gatehouse before him, and Yves coming forward to meet him. Yves knew better than to press for details, but Tristan gave him the basics: "It's over, Yves. We won." And then he looked ahead, to the wide oak doors that would lead him to his family.

"MATTHIEU, LOOK, THERE are lots of ripe strawberries. Come and try some."

Matthieu DesChênes glanced over at his mother where she knelt among the low plants. He didn't know why she liked to be in the garden so much. Matthieu's father, Dominic, would be king one day. His mama could have servants bring her strawberries anytime she wanted, but there she was, pulling them off their stems and holding them out enticingly.

Matthieu liked strawberries, though, so he joined his mother and filled his mouth with the succulent fruits. A dribble of red juice escaped his lips, and Justine wiped it away with her thumb and smiled. "Yummy, aren't they?" Matthieu nodded, but he wasn't thinking about strawberries. He was thinking about the war. He leaned over and carefully disgorged the red, runny pulp onto the inside of his wrist.

"Matthieu! What in the world—?"

"If I got wounded in the war, it would look like this," he said, admiring the effect. "But if your whole arm got cut off, that would be blood everywhere, wouldn't it Mama?"

He had gone too far. He could tell by the way Justine's face became closed in and hard. "That is enough, young sir! This is no kind of talk for a five-year-old boy." She pulled a hankie from her skirt pocket and scrubbed the red stain from his arm.

"Mama." Matthieu's voice had gone all choky and quiet. It meant he might cry. He hated to cry, but he couldn't help it. Justine heard, and her face softened. Her hands became gentle, smoothing open his clenched fingers.

"What's wrong, then?"

"I want them to come home: Grandpa, and Uncle Tristan and Gabrielle."

Matthieu still didn't know exactly what the war was or where it was. But he knew he didn't like how quiet and empty the castle was, how the grown-ups were always talking together in low, worried voices and then giving him pretend smiles when they saw him, like the ones painted on the faces on the dumbshow players that he saw last winter. He didn't really like thinking about swords cutting off arms, either.

"Oh, lovey." Justine knelt and held him close. "We all do.

We just have to keep hoping they will come back soon. And safe." Matthieu nestled against his mother's shoulder, but his eyes, curious and alert as ever, were drawn to the gatehouse. Old Yves was talking to somebody.

Matthieu squinted as a figure came into view. Maybe it was another messenger.

TRISTAN HAD TAKEN only a few steps across the courtyard when a small shape came arrowing toward him over the broad lawn. Matthieu didn't stop running until he barreled into Tristan's legs and wrapped both arms tight around his uncle's thighs.

"Whoa, boy! You're going to knock me right over!"

The boy gazed up with shining eyes. "Uncle Tris! Is the war over? Did you win? I'm five now, and look!" He grasped his lower lip and pulled it down to his chin. "I lost a tooth!"

Matthieu's chatter stopped as he took in Tristan's plaster cast. Silent, eyes wide, he touched it with a tentative finger. "Did you get your arm chopped off?"

Tristan guffawed, a heartfelt laugh that made him feel, for a moment, that perhaps nothing had changed after all, that the banners had every reason to fly gay and carefree in the sun. He ruffled Matthieu's brown hair. "No, Matthieu. It's just a break, and Gabrielle fixed it. When she takes off the plaster, I'll be right as rain."

"Ohhh," the boy breathed, looking, Tristan thought, just a little disappointed.

But Tristan's attention had turned back to the doorway, opening even now. It was time. He bent down to the tousled head. "I have to go talk to your grandma now, Matthieu," he said gently.

He watched as his family emerged onto the landing:

Justine, holding her daughter Madeleine by the hand, guiding her to one side to make room for Solange; Dominic hovering protectively behind. Tristan drew a deep breath. "Help me find the words, Gabi." The whisper was a kind of prayer. He wished his sister were beside him now—she would know how to do this right.

Tristan strode up the long walkway and folded his mother into his arms.

GABRIELLE WOULD HAVE given almost anything to be at Tristan's side at that moment—but not a man's life. One of the wounded soldiers had spiked a raging fever in the night and lay too ill even to swallow the bonemender's herbals. Gabrielle's unique skills were his last recourse, and so she put aside regret and spent the day beside her patient in a rattling cart, pushing back the infection that threatened to overwhelm him.

By the next morning, when Verdeau's soldiers marched into Chênier at last, her patient was out of danger. All around them, people were cheering, worried loved ones straining to catch sight of the sons and husbands and brothers to whom they had bid farewell a season ago. And there was Solange, clapping and waving for the troops, never again to stand with her husband by her side. The sight of her—a small, erect figure flanked by her two grown sons—all but broke Gabrielle's heart.

"I can't stand this. I have to go to her," Gabrielle said to Féolan.

"Go," he urged. "You are no soldier. Are you bound to linger here, awaiting dismissal?"

"I guess not. You, either." She glanced up at the tall Elf walking at her side. She had not questioned his decision to make the journey home with her, only accepted it gladly. They belonged together now.

"Yet I will stay. Your mother needs family now, not a guest."

And she had pushed through the thick ranks of men and taken her place with the DesChênes family—her family, always, whatever her actual parentage. Gabrielle could only imagine the effort of will that allowed Solange to stand so straight and composed on the high dais set up in the mustering grounds, welcoming the returning soldiers, praising their victory and sending her own condolences to those who had lost loved ones.

Only later, in their own home, had Solange allowed an embrace and the tears that must follow. And then, ensconced with Gabrielle in her chamber, Solange had insisted on the full, painful telling of Jerome's death.

"He suffered very little, Mama," Gabrielle ended miserably. "That much comfort I can give you."

"More than that, my love," assured her mother. "He died in his daughter's arms, not alone, and though it was appallingly foolish of you to take that risk, I will be forever grateful for it." She took Gabrielle's hands in her own and squeezed them. "You go on downstairs now." Her lips were trembling, but she shooed Gabrielle away. "You have guests to see to, I think. And a story of your own to tell, by the looks of it, which I will ask for tomorrow."

DERKH WAS ALREADY tucked into bed in Gabrielle's little clinic, with Féolan in attendance.

"Just like old times," Féolan remarked, as she stepped into the room. He had spent a good part of the previous summer in that same clinic, watching over his friend Danaïs's recovery.

Gabrielle stood in the doorway and let her eyes roam over the familiar shelves and cabinets, the four neat beds, the bright windows. Once, she thought, this orderly clean space had represented her image of a bonemender's work: helping people through illness and the natural cycle of birth and death, the occasional setting of a bone or stitching of an accidental cut—not struggling in a sea of gore and filth to keep a man's guts from spilling out of his body. It seemed a quaint little refuge now.

"This is where you live?" Derkh's abrupt question cut short her reverie.

"Yes," she replied, wondering at the tension in the young Greffaire's voice.

"But this is the castle," he said, pointing out the obvious. "Are you the Royal Surgeon?"

Féolan laughed. "Gabrielle, you've misled the lad. Confess, girl!"

Gabrielle caught Derkh's anxious confusion and was instantly remorseful. "This is my family home," she explained. "When I was your father's prisoner, I didn't want him to know who I was. And when we met up again later, after the battle, I never thought to tell you. King Jerome was my father." And even that was not the whole truth, because she was someone else now, wasn't she? But it seemed more than enough for Derkh, who was shaking his head in disbelief.

"Derkh," she said, smiling as she pulled up a chair beside the bed. "I am not a different person because of my family."

The young Greffaire considered this statement in baffled silence. Then he looked up at Gabrielle, dark eyes nearly black against the white pillow. "In my country you would be."

CHAPTER TWO

TRISTAN, his face set in a solemn mask, stared out over the bowed heads of the crowd. Verdeau's regents, high officials and noble families had traveled from every corner of the country to attend King Jerome's funeral rites; the Great Hall was packed tight with mourners and stiflingly hot.

What is wrong with me? he wondered. He had felt restless since his return home, as if an uneasy beast were pent up inside him, pacing back and forth in its confinement. He lay awake night after night, a new and unwelcome experience for a man who had always slept soundly, even on the ground in the Krylian foothills. And now here he was, unable to concentrate on his own father's funeral. He tried to find some meaning in the long, dismal service, or at least from standing with his family and with the people of his country, to honor Jerome's memory. But he could not grasp onto the stream of words or close the distance that set him apart from those he loved.

Afterward, an endless line of well-wishers filed past to greet the royal family. Tristan and his family stood in formal order: first his mother, Solange, erect and gracious despite the exhaustion she must feel; then his older brother, Dominic, Regent of the Blanchette Coast, and Dominic's wife Justine; and Gabrielle, so different from Tristan with her mysterious insights and abilities, yet so close to him too. By the time they make it to me at the end of the line, he thought, they are probably as tired of the whole business as I am.

Tristan had always connected effortlessly with people from all walks of life. Today, though, was almost more than he could endure. An hour crept by, more, and still he was grasping hands, nodding politely, mouthing platitudes. His eyes swept down the visitation line—still so many people—and came to rest on a tall, slightly stooped form and gray head just visible above the crowd. André Martineau of Blanchette. Rosalie's father.

It was like awakening from a foggy dream. For several anxious moments his view was blocked. Then André stepped forward, and Tristan caught a glimpse of Rosalie's dark head and pink cheek. She came, he thought, and his heart tripped into a canter, mourning or no.

Tristan had left for the war without telling Rosalie how he felt about her—without even telling himself. But all the way home she had hung in his thoughts—a small, dark-haired, high-spirited girl with laughing brown eyes and round pink cheeks. Now, from a single glimpse, he realized what had been eating at his heart.

The line inched along until at last he was shaking André's hand, murmuring his thanks at the words of condolence. And then Rosalie stood before him, her eyes welling with tears. "Tristan, I'm so sorry."

He didn't hesitate. He wrapped his arms around her in a bear hug, despite the crowd of onlookers, and held on for dear life. "Rosie," he whispered. "Rosie, I'm so glad you're here." Her answering squeeze made it clear she was glad too. He released her, keeping hold of one hand. Such a small, neat hand. "Will you be staying for a while?" he asked. "Promise you won't run back to Blanchette without telling me, like last time. I need to talk to you."

DERKH SAT IN the little garden outside Gabrielle's clinic, legs extended, head tipped back to the warm spring sun. He appeared relaxed, but his belly was tight with anxiety. As Derkh's wound healed and his strength returned, worries for the future had begun to trouble him. What was he doing here? He was a Greffaire soldier. That Gabrielle had first healed and then befriended him did not change that fact. By rights, he should be a prisoner, not a guest.

A creak of hinges interrupted his brooding thoughts; craning his neck, he saw Gabrielle step through the clinic door behind him.

"Hi," he said, the word feeling strange in his mouth. There was no real equivalent in Greffaire: either the greeting was more formal, addressed to a superior, or omitted altogether. "Come to check me again?"

Even in her plain mourning dress she looked radiant, and her quick smile washed over him like sunshine.

"I'll take a look, yes, if I may. But unless you've had an unexpected setback, I'm thinking it's time for you to stop being a patient. I'm having a room prepared for you upstairs, and you can take your meals with us from now on."

Derkh's face flushed dark. Here was something he had not expected. It had been shock enough to discover that Gabrielle was, in fact, of Verdeau's royal family and to find himself in their very castle. Yet the DesChênes family, including the queen herself, had shown him nothing but kindness. Derkh's family was of high enough rank in his own country, but even his father Col, who as high commander of the armed forces certainly attended tactical meetings with the emperor, would never have lodged in the palace nor spoken with the emperor's family. Derkh was well aware that his fate would have been different indeed had the situation been reversed and he a Verdeau soldier captured in Greffier. At first he had been too full of dazed gratitude to feel anything else.

But this. To eat with them, and while they mourned for the king his own people had killed—it was unthinkable.

He didn't know how to respond. He didn't understand Verdeau protocol, the manners and conventions that lay behind his hosts' easy manners. He only knew he must refuse.

"I think I should eat in the kitchen, with the servants," he mumbled. That would be bad enough: all of them knowing where he came from, reminded of it every time he opened his mouth to speak, tolerating him only because of Gabrielle's protection.

For a moment Gabrielle looked as though she had been slapped. Derkh hated himself for causing that look. Then she covered it with a warm concern he wished he could deflect. "If that's what you want, Derkh, of course," she said. Not happy, though hiding it. "But you are our guest, and more than welcome at our table. I wish you would join us."

"I can't," he said. "Gabrielle, I can't. Your mother. She should not have to…" Make polite talk with her dead husband's enemy over breakfast, he thought, and could not find less vicious words to say.

Gabrielle's calm voice rescued him. "It's all right. I'll tell the cook to make a place for you and to let you know when meal-times are." And then changing the subject: "Why don't you take that bandage off and let the air at your skin? I'll come back in an hour or so to redo it."

She hesitated at the door to the clinic, turned back to face him.

"Derkh…I know it must be awkward for you here. But give it time. Things will work out."

Will they? he wondered. How?

IN TRUTH, QUEEN Solange no more thought of Derkh as the enemy responsible for Jerome's death than she would a Greffaire warhorse. She saw only an abandoned, sick boy, and her immediate instinct had been to gather him into the fold. She asked about him at dinner that night.

"I thought Derkh might join us tonight."

"I offered," Gabrielle said, still puzzled. "He seemed alarmed at the prospect. He asked to eat in the kitchen."

"Maybe because we are in mourning," Solange suggested. Jerome's funeral rites were only a few days past, and his absence at the table still loomed large over their meals.

"Yeah, he's what, maybe fifteen years old?" offered Tristan, his words emerging—barely—through a large mouthful of pheasant. Gabrielle didn't necessarily want this view of his half-chewed dinner, but she was glad to see that her brother's legendary appetite had returned. She'd been a bit worried about him. "When I was his age, I wouldn't have wanted to sit with a bunch of strangers who just had a funeral. I'd have been afraid they'd be weeping all the time, and me not knowing what to do."

Tristan had, in fact, done his share of weeping over Jerome's death, including at mealtime. But his sense of loss was changing now into something less sharp, something held more quietly in the heart.

"Mama, Uncle Tristan is talking with his mouth full," Madeleine pointed out. Tristan crossed his eyes at her and opened his mouth as wide as it would go, giving her such a cavernous view that Madeleine's prim smirk dissolved into helpless giggling.

"Yes, Madeleine, and it's equally rude to point out other people's mistakes," replied Justine, doing her best to ignore Tristan's antics.

"You might try that little trick with Rosalie, Tris," suggested Dominic. "It's sure to impress her."

Gabrielle joined in the laughter, but her mind circled back to Derkh. She wished she could talk to Féolan about the boy's growing unhappiness. Oddly enough, he seemed to have a closer rapport with Derkh than any of them.

But Féolan was riding north, to his home in the Elvish settlement of Stonewater. "There will be a lament for our own fallen," he had explained to Gabrielle. "I may already have missed it, but I must try. I do not even know who has been lost and who lives."

CHAPTER THREE

TRISTAN'S eyes followed the watercourse of the Avine River as far south as he could see. Somewhere beyond the limits of his vision lay Blanchette and the ocean.

"It's long since I've been to the coast," he mused. "In my memory, the wind is always blowing. I remember feeling it would catch my clothes and lift me into the air like a kite."

Rosalie and Tristan had ridden south to a lookout terrace that jutted out over the river some miles from Chênier. They had picnicked and chatted and teased each other, and if Tristan did not speak soon he would find himself back in the castle and this carefully engineered opportunity wasted.

Rosalie smiled. "You were smaller then, I expect. Though I still feel I might be carried off when the gale blows hard. But on calm days, the sun sparkles on the sea like a thousand diamonds. That makes up for the wind."

"That's how I feel when I look at you," said Tristan, "like I might be carried off."

He turned to her then, his blue eyes serious and searching. "Rosie, perhaps I should not speak of this in a time of mourning. But I know my father would take no offense, and I cannot wait longer. It has been in my heart for so long."

Tristan paused, disconcerted at how difficult he was finding this. It was like leaping over a cliff, not knowing whether deep

water or jutting rock lay at the bottom. Just say it, man. He
steeled himself and tried again. "All the way home from the war
I thought of you, of how badly I wanted to be with you," he said,
"*needed* to be with you. I was desperate with it. And at my father's
funeral, when I saw you there...it saved me. I love you, Rosie. I
know your father is not... He thinks I'm irresponsible, not serious
enough. But I'm not. I mean I am. I know what it means to be
a family. And I—"

A small hand covered his mouth, cutting off his words. Brown
eyes that sparkled like the sun on the sea held his.

"Yes. If what you're trying to do is ask me to marry you, then
yes—though I could grow gray as my father waiting for you to
spit it out!"

STOPPING BY THE kitchen to speak to the cook, Gabrielle was
surprised to see Derkh in the scullery, scrubbing out cook pots.
She raised her eyebrows questioningly at the cook.

"Oh, him. I thought he was terrible snooty at first, you know.
He never spoke a word to the one of us. But after a few days, he
come to me private and asked if I had work he could do. I reckon
he's just shy to speak with that horrid thick tongue of his. Not
much wonder, either."

"No," said Gabrielle. "Not much wonder." Poor Derkh, she
thought. I've been a neglectful host. There had been little time
for entertaining anyone, and in fairness Derkh had made himself
scarce since his discharge from the little infirmary. Still she felt a
stab of remorse to find him up to the elbows in dishwater. Yet...she
was proud of him too. Honest work was healthier than idleness.

"Can you tell Derkh?" she asked the cook. "Not now—after
I've gone." She didn't know if it would shame him to be seen

playing the pot-boy, and she wasn't about to find out. "Just say I was looking for him and would like to speak with him. Tell him I'll be in the clinic for the next while."

DERKH EDGED INTO the little clinic and stood just inside the door. He felt ill at ease everywhere in Chênier, even with Gabrielle. She treated him just as she always had, like an equal. But for Derkh, her rank—and his—had opened a chasm between them so wide it was a struggle to speak across it.

"Did you want to see me, Gabrielle?"

"Hi, Derkh." Gabrielle bent over the bottles she was filling and labeling. "I've hardly caught sight of you lately. You know, things have been so busy around here I'm afraid I've left you to fend for yourself."

"I don't mind."

"Well, I wanted to ask you for a favor. I'm riding up into the hills tomorrow to gather herbs. Would you come and help? Mother worries when I go into the woods alone, and I don't want to ask Tristan. I know he's hoping to see Rosalie."

Derkh hesitated, but the prospect of a ride and an afternoon away from the complexities of life in Chênier was too much to resist. "Sure. I'd like to."

"Great. Meet me at the stables right after lunch. All right?"

Derkh nodded, then frowned. What if he arrived before Gabrielle and was questioned? Would they believe he had business with royalty? Would they even understand his speech? Just picturing it made his teeth clench. "Uh, can you tell someone at the stable I am coming?" he asked. "So I don't have to explain why I am there?"

"Of course." She looked down at her work once again, but

Derkh had the uneasy feeling she was really looking inside of him. Her question, though, was casual. "Are they feeding you all right?"

"Sure," he said. "The food is good. That cook, she looks mean, but she's all right."

Gabrielle smiled. "She used to make a great show of scolding Tristan when he was little and then slip him sweets and treats under the table. It was a little game—anything he wanted, as long as he didn't ruin her reputation for an evil temper."

Derkh laughed, and things became easy between them for a bit. "Our cook was something like that too," he said. "Maybe it runs in their blood."

THEY HAD WORKED for a good hour before Gabrielle broached any serious talk.

"Derkh, how is it for you here?" she asked. Her eyes, the green of a forest pool, rested on him.

His gaze slid away to scan the horizon. "I'm very grateful for everything," he said. "People have been very kind."

She waved a grubby hand impatiently. "I'm not fishing for gratitude. Look, you and I have been through too much together to resort to polite lies now." This time his eyes met hers. He had been in agonizing pain from a sword to the gut, and Gabrielle on the verge of collapse, when his father had thrust her into Derkh's tent in the Greffaire camp. Commander Col had offered his prisoner a bargain: her life in exchange for his son's. The bargain had meant nothing to Gabrielle, but the suffering of a boy too young to have taken such a wound called to her healer's heart. In the grueling effort to pull him back from the brink of death, an unlikely friendship had been born.

Gabrielle pondered the coincidence or fate that had brought them together a second time. Derkh, abandoned by the retreating Greffaires, had been found by the Elvish army, his wound infected, his life once more in danger. They had called on Féolan to translate, and Féolan, putting two and two together, had taken Derkh straight to Gabrielle's healing tent. She had not thought twice about caring for him—and bringing him home—alongside Verdeau's wounded.

"I'm asking as a friend," said Gabrielle. "I can see you are troubled. Will you not speak your mind to me?"

Derkh groped for words. "It's just…what happens next? I know I am lucky just to be alive, but what am I to do now? I don't see it."

"You will always be welcome with us, Derkh."

"But I cannot always be the pet Greffaire, lounging around the royal castle of Verdeau." The words sounded harsh in his Greffaire dialect.

Gabrielle rocked back on her heels and considered him. She had thought of Derkh as a boy, she realized, when in Greffier he had already taken on the role of a man. And his life had been ordered, defined. Now he had no place. "In strange seas without a compass," she murmured and smiled at the memory.

"My father used to say that," she explained, and was sorry to see him wince. "Derkh, you did not kill my father," she said firmly. "You cannot take my every fond reminiscence as an accusation of guilt."

"Sorry," he muttered. "He was right, though. That is how I feel."

"Do you have any training? In a trade or skill, I mean?"

"My father was the commander of the armed forces. I was trained for war," he said bleakly. "I can hardly go join your army."

"No. And I can hardly promise you a rank to match your father's.

But I thought that with a trade you could at least be your own master and not under the thumb of an evil-tempered cook."

He looked startled. "You know about that?"

"Yes. And it was well done, to offer your labor."

They worked in silence for a while. Then Derkh, with a visible effort, spoke up again.

"You will marry Féolan and live with him, won't you? In Stonewater."

Gabrielle blinked. "Yes," she said. "We will not wed, probably, until next summer, about a year from now. But this year I will spend the late summer and autumn there, and the winter here with my mother."

"I was just wondering. I don't want to be any bother. But...well, I wondered if I might come along. It's not right for me to be in the castle, now I'm not sick or anything, but with the way I talk I can't really...," he trailed off, red-faced. Gabrielle could see how much it had cost him to make the request.

"Derkh, if it was only up to me I would say 'yes' without even thinking about it," she began.

"That's all right," he said hastily. "I understand."

"No, you don't. You had better let me finish. Féolan would welcome you too, I am sure. But Stonewater is an isolated community. They keep their presence almost secret, and I do not know them well enough to know if there are rules about bringing visitors. I only hesitate because we might have to get permission first."

"Oh," he said. "I didn't realize. We walked all through La Maronne and half of Verdeau without a single checkpoint, so I thought..."

"You thought right. We have free access in and out of our towns.

But the Elves keep themselves separate from us. Until the Greffaire invasion, most people didn't even know they existed."

Now he was openly confused. "What did you call them?"

Gabrielle realized her oversight. Of course he doesn't understand, she thought. He was feverish and ill through the invasion and long afterward.

She started again. "Derkh, Féolan is not Human. He and his people are Elves. I am half-Elf myself, as it turns out. My parents adopted me as a foundling, and they never suspected I was…" Her voice trailed away. Gabrielle still could not think of herself as "not Human."

"Elves… *Aelvich?*" He laughed. "What, the unseen people of children's tales who steal things and fly away on the mist?"

"They may have become that in the lore of your people," said Gabrielle. "In real life they are like Féolan. It was an Elvish army that came upon your forces from the rear."

Derkh's expression changed to wonder. "The tall, silent warriors. And the men who found me in the cart," he said. "I can picture them now. They did look different."

Gabrielle nodded. "You don't notice it so much when there is only one. If you go to Stonewater, you will see… But Derkh, here is the thing: They don't speak Krylaise, not even a variation. Their language is entirely different. If it is permitted, you can come and stay with us as long as you like. It is a good place to heal and think. But I do not think you will find a real home there."

CHAPTER FOUR

A single, haunting voice soared over the dark waters of the lake, sending the opening bars of the *Lament for the Dead* to meet the rising moon. Amplified by the water and the stillness of the night, the sound seemed to rise out of the silver light of the moonbeam itself.

Two thousand and more Elves stood strung along the shoreline, yet the silence was unbroken but for that clear, sorrowful voice. Féolan let the music wash through him. It sank into them all, linking soul to soul so that when at last the lament swelled with the voices of the full choir it was as though the pain and the beauty were pouring forth from every person there. Long they sang. The moon rode high in a sky full of stars before the haunting music died away, leaving behind one liquid line of melody that floated out over the water and faded into the night.

Though many faces shone with tears and some among the bereaved sobbed openly, the silence held. The naming of the fallen, the paying of respects, had all been seen to earlier. But it was the lament that most truly spoke their sorrow and most deeply comforted. Now, as they made their way back along the shadowy pathways of Moonwash settlement, none wished to break the spell it had woven.

Féolan walked with his parents to their dwelling. They had much to speak of together—but not this night. He embraced them wordlessly and slipped off to bed, to his own memories and dreams.

THE NEXT MORNING Féolan began the long retelling of his adventures. "But I will say before I start," he said, "that the story ends in a betrothal, and that the match is not so ill as it will seem at first.

"Nay, you must have patience!" he laughed, staying his mother's questions. "I tell you this only to forestall your fears, but I will not go so far as to make a mishmash of my tale. If you want to know, you must listen all the way through."

They were settled into deep reedweave chairs on the verandah that in good weather became a sun-dappled extension of the house. A bold chipmunk made a foray under their feet, searching for stray crumbs. It dashed off in alarm when Shéovar tossed it a crust, only to freeze mid-flight, return, and stuff the morsel into its cheeks. Féolan watched the saucy creature absently as he gathered his thoughts.

He began with the scouting foray into the mountains—nearly a year ago now—and the unexpected discovery of the *Gref Orisé* camp. "Really, there was no reason to even go that way, except that a couple of the scouts had an urge to see the high country," he confessed. "We never expected to encounter a soul." Then came his journey with Danaïs down the Gamier Road and then cross-country south through Verdeau, the disastrous boar attack that ripped open his companion's thigh, and their desperate arrival at Castle DesChênes. "And that's where I met Gabrielle," he concluded. "I will need another cup of this tea to tell the next part."

Step by step it unfolded: their growing love, Gabrielle's appalled refusal of him when she learned of the difference in their life spans,

his reckless spying mission into *Gref Oris*. By the time he told
of the Elvish raid on the *Gref Orisé* war camp and how they had
unwittingly rescued Gabrielle, the day was warm and Lunala was
dabbing at her eyes. As Féolan's story wound to a close—the successful alliance of the Elves with the Human forces, and Gabrielle's
discovery, in Stonewater, of her true ancestry—she came to him
and kissed him on both cheeks, her gaze warm and joyful.

"Brave hearts, both, to walk through such fire and find each
other at journey's end," she said. "I am glad beyond words for
you, my son."

But Shéovar did not speak, and his eyes were troubled.

"So then, Father, what is it?" asked Féolan. "I promise you will
like her."

"I doubt it not," said Shéovar. "I like her already, from your
words alone. But Féolan, she is not yet thirty."

"I know. I know, but she seems older. Remember, she has been
a full adult in Verdeau for a decade—and that is much longer to
Humans than to us. Though she is half-Elven, her…what?…her
frame of reference, you might say, is entirely Human. Father, if
you are suggesting we wait to wed, she will not wish it. Among
men, she is nearly past the age of marrying!"

Shéovar looked skeptical. The swift cycle of Human life was
difficult for one who had not walked among Humans to understand.

"Féolan, there is another thing that worries me, and it is not easy
for me to say this to you. From what you tell me, you are the first
Elf she has ever known. I see how deeply you love her and that
you are resolved to bear the heartache of her early death. But is
it fair to claim her pledge now? I cannot but wonder: might not
a young girl feel herself in love with a stranger who sweeps into

her life and strikes a deep chord of recognition, understands her perhaps in ways no one else ever has? If Gabrielle were to discover, in time, that it was not you in yourself, but the deep pull of our race that called her, if she came to realize that another could have matched her heart better, none could blame her. Yet it would be a sorrow to you both, nonetheless."

The very thought was harrowing. Féolan could find no words to answer his father. Almost he hated him for having raised such a specter. And yet…forcing himself to look square at the thing, uncolored by his own desire, it was an obvious concern. It shamed him that he had not once questioned how circumstances had pushed Gabrielle into his arms.

She is no moonstruck girl, he told himself. She knows her own heart. But the doubt remained.

There were no answers in the depths of the translucent tea cup, nor in the compassionate eyes of his parents. Féolan rose to his feet abruptly, half-raised his hand to ward off further words. "I need a walk," he said and strode off toward the water.

DISGUSTING. DERKH EYED the pork scraps and potato skins floating on the viscid surface of the washtub, dipped them out with his fingers and flung them into the garbage. The royal family had, by the looks of it, fed a mighty number of people after the memorial services for Verdeau's dead, and grief had not dinted the guests' appetites. His dishwater had grown tepid and gray with grease, the washing running ahead of the hot water supply. He would have to wait on the fire. Derkh dragged the tin tub out the door and across the dirt yard to the ditch, where he tipped out the old dishwater. Pushing the sweaty hair off his forehead, he let the evening breeze play on his hot skin.

"Derkh."

He looked up. It was the cook, and her sharp eye made him feel instantly guilty.

"Sorry," he said, embarrassed as always by his awkward speech. "I wait for the new water."

"That's all right. I was going to say, why not run off now and let Jonas finish up? By the time he's done with the floor, the water will be hot."

"I can finish," he protested, but she cut him off.

"It's Jonas's job. It's good of you to help, and the heavens know we can use you, but you don't have to stay till moonrise. That's for the likes of us as gets paid to do it."

Should he insist, or did she want to be rid of him? He couldn't tell. Nodding abruptly, Derkh did as he was told. But he wasn't about to go back to his room, not until the hallways were empty for the night. He didn't want to meet up with anyone on the day of the Verdeau memorial.

Instead, he hopped the ditch, climbed the rail fence that closed off the kitchen and laundry yard and crossed the wide lawn behind the castle. A small unattended door in the stone wall that enclosed the castle grounds led to a footpath that wound up into the hills. Broad and gentle at first, it soon narrowed and rose steeply. Derkh climbed hard, pushing himself to go faster until his breath grew ragged and painful and the flesh behind his scar flared in protest with each step. By the time the late spring sun began to dip behind the line of hills, he was high enough to see the land for miles around glow under the last glances of rosy light and then darken into shadow. But he did not see, because he was crying—sobbing hoarsely with each gasping breath as he hadn't since he was a child on his mother's knee. Finally, legs, belly and lungs all burning with exertion, he flung himself on the ground and gave himself up to it.

He cried for his own dead: for all the men he had trained, lived and fought with, if not befriended; for the father he had feared and sometimes hated and loved with all his heart. He cried from the constant strain of being an outsider, and although he did not cry with longing for his homeland, by the time the tears were spent he had decided. He did not belong here. He would go back to Greffier.

CHAPTER FIVE

TRISTAN and Rosalie sat on the stone bench in the center of the garden, drawing out their last night together. In the morning, she and her father would return to Blanchette.

Their courtship was official now. Solange had welcomed the news, as Tristan had known she would. André too, had given his immediate, if somewhat restrained, blessing. His agreement had left Tristan feeling slightly deflated, like a child who has prepared a great list of compelling reasons why he should have a treat, only to be given it before he asks. He wondered if his role in the war had elevated him in André's eyes.

"I couldn't shake the idea, after the last battle," confessed Tristan, "that you would be married to someone else by the time I got back. It drove me crazy."

"Actually, I did have one offer, from a very rich man. He owns half of Blanchette." Rosalie's tone was cool, considering. One look at Tristan's stricken face and she relented. "He was horrible, Tris. I never missed you more than when I was enduring his company!"

"You little vixen, to torture me so!" Tristan flipped down his lower lip, squinted up his eyes and leered at her while a string of drool escaped his mouth and trickled to his chin. "Yuuu mush pay…whish a KHISSH!" He pounced. Rosalie squealed and struggled—but only until his face rearranged itself. She was happy, then, to make amends for her teasing.

"I will come to the coast as soon as I can," promised Tristan. "There is still a lot to do here—you know, this war may not be over. There could be a second invasion, this summer or next year. We've left sizeable sentry forces guarding the passes, but we need to bring all four Basin countries into a common defense plan. Work more closely with the Elves too, I hope. Once we get things organized, Dominic will move his family back to Blanchette—and I'll come along for a visit."

"Work hard, then, and come soon," said Rosalie.

They spoke but little after that, though the moon had traveled the sky and set before they walked the deserted streets back to Rosalie's lodging.

ROSALIE HAD NO urge to recount to Tristan the details of her encounter with Pierre LaBarque. She was just grateful it had become a thing she could joke about.

Early in the spring, perhaps two weeks after the Verdeau army had begun its march north to the Skyway Pass, her father had received a visit from LaBarque, a wealthy merchant who traded in everything from Gamier fleece and textiles to the precious ores and salt of Barilles. In his mid-forties, still active and healthy, LaBarque had been on a trade voyage to Gamier at the time of the muster and thus missed the call to arms.

As niceties were exchanged, the topic of war inevitably arose. LaBarque shrugged. "It will turn out to be a fool's errand, this great mobilization," he pronounced. His deep slow voice gave each word weight, as though he were delivering a speech. "Meanwhile, I gather they have left us all but defenseless here on the coast, where the threat from sea raids is real. One can hardly believe our king has ties to Crow Island, given the way he neglects our interests."

Rosalie had flushed red. Eyes wide, she had looked to her father to dispute this unfair condemnation. But if André shared her outrage he gave no sign. Always careful of speech, he looked mildly surprised, but said nothing.

LaBarque's next topic of conversation was more shocking still. He turned to Rosalie's father—never addressing her at all—and requested his consideration "as a suitable husband for your lovely daughter, Rosalie." As coldly as though discussing a business transaction, he went on to detail his extensive holdings, the worth of his home and the solidity of his many investments, concluding, "I could most certainly promise your daughter a most comfortable and secure existence."

Beyond speech, Rosalie stared at her lap and listened while André thanked the man graciously and assured him of their respect and esteem. "I will have to discuss this with Rosalie, of course," he concluded.

LaBarque rose to his feet. "Well then," he said briskly, "I leave you to it." At the front door he paused, reached for Rosalie's hand, puckered out his thin lips and kissed it with an awkward flourish. "We will want to know each other better," he said. "Please dine with me at my home, a week hence. I will send a carriage at six."

André interrupted. "Well, now, Pierre—"

LaBarque fixed his dark eyes on Rosalie's father. "My dear André, you are not worried about the lack of chaperone?" He appeared amused. "I am not some wild young man. Such is the advantage of a mature suitor, surely. I give you my word she will be delivered safely home, say by ten bells?"

The door closed. Rosalie gave a sigh of relief. "Thank goodness he's gone!" she exclaimed, looking back with a giggle. To her consternation, her father did not smile back.

"Rosalie," he said, "Lord LaBarque has made a serious proposal, and you would be wise to consider it carefully. He is a very influential man."

"He is too old!" she blurted out. "And his manner is, oh, awful! You can't be serious."

"Of course I am serious!" André snapped. He softened and tried again. "Rosalie, you know what I want for you is your happiness. I cannot and will not force you to marry. But I ask you not to dismiss this man on the basis of a fleeting first impression. I believe he has much to offer you."

"But Tristan—"

"What about Tristan?" her father said bluntly. "Did he speak of marriage when we were last in Chênier?"

"No, but... Well, you hustled us away so quickly he wouldn't have had time."

"If he had really intended to, he would have made the time," said André. "You have to think of the long term. A charming smile and a royal title do not make a good solid husband."

"There is more to Tristan than that!" Rosalie flared, tears now pricking at her eyes. Her father, always a serious man, had become almost severe since her mother's death five years ago. Rosalie, his youngest and his only unmarried child, thought longingly of the days when her mother and older sisters had filled the house with talk and laughter.

"Perhaps there is. I confess I have not seen it. Be that as it may, I ask you to go to dinner with Lord LaBarque and to keep your options open." His voice grew gentle, and the words hurt all the more: "Rosalie, if there is an invasion—and in this I believe Pierre will be proved wrong—you cannot be sure of your Tristan returning. I am sorry to say it, but such is the harshness of war."

So Rosalie had gone to dinner and made a dutiful effort to be gracious, but she could do nothing about the skin-crawling aversion she felt to Lord LaBarque.

He had taken her arm and toured her through room after room of his massive town house before sitting her in a dark, velvet-draped parlor. Like the rest of the home, it was richly appointed, even sumptuous, but gloomy and close. No breath of the new spring air had been allowed to enter here. Rosalie asked politely about LaBarque's business—which obviously pleased him and led to a rather long accounting of his many financial ventures—and then about his "other interests," which elicited only a blank stare. Serious men, the look seemed to imply, do not indulge in such frivolity.

After a long, awkward silence LaBarque asked, "And you? Do you have 'interests'?"

"Well," said Rosalie, "I love range archery, have done since I had my first lesson as a young girl. I hold the women's championship for this area, actually."

This time the silence was distinctly disapproving. "I deem," LaBarque pronounced at last, "that the arts of war ill become a woman's hand."

At that moment a maid appeared, saving Rosalie the burden of a reply, and requested their presence in the dining room. As LaBarque armed her to the table, Rosalie let her mind wander to the time she had bested Tristan in a shooting match and been rewarded with his delighted laugh and the ceremonial presentation of his behind to kick. Oh, Tris, come home safe, she prayed. Though rumor of fighting had reached the coast, no official news had been heard.

Dinner crawled on, both tedious and nerve-racking. With the last course—apple dumplings and tiny glasses of syrupy liqueur—LaBarque turned, as she had known he would, to the matter of marriage.

Rosalie had prepared her speech beforehand and delivered it carefully: "Lord LaBarque, I am most honored by your interest in my hand. But my heart is now in the keeping of another, and until I know how things stand with him, I do not feel free to consider marriage. I beg your pardon and your patience."

Though his expression did not appear to change, a cold anger settled over LaBarque's hawk-like face. The effect was so unsettling that Rosalie felt her skin draw up in ghost-flesh, as though the room had grown colder.

"Another," he sneered. "That would be our dashing young princeling, off playing at war, I suppose? I'd be surprised if he even remembers who you are."

Speechless with anger and humiliation, Rosalie set her lips together, determined not to give LaBarque the satisfaction of seeing her upset. There were rules for this kind of discussion, she raged to herself, and not even the most boorish country oaf would indulge in such insults.

LaBarque's eyes narrowed, and his cold voice cut like a whip. "I am not accustomed to giving up my treasures to anyone, let alone royal brats who think the world is their toy. Nor will I hang meekly at the feet of a little fool who does not know her own best interest. I suggest you take just enough time to reconsider the reality of your position and not wait around for your young gallant to trade you for a Maronnaise princess!"

LaBarque did not accompany her on the coach ride home, to Rosalie's enormous relief. She had disliked the man from the moment she set eyes on him. Now she knew why.

CHAPTER SIX

UN on her eyelids, the warble and trill of birdsong, the fresh scent of a summer woodland on a teasing breeze. Gabrielle stretched and lingered in her bed, savoring the slow awakening of her senses.

She was home. It was a new home, but from the moment she had set foot into Stonewater, just three days ago, she had been at ease. Full of excited recognition and gladness at each new sight, she realized with surprise that she had missed it. Not just Féolan, but the place itself—the subtle, airy buildings, the mingling of wood and bright glades, the winding pathways. Then little Eleara had flown down the path to meet her, no longer shy but chattering brightly, and Danaïs and Célani had followed, and she could hardly remember the awkwardness of her first visit.

The only mar to her happiness was on Derkh's behalf. She had been surprised to find he still wanted to come to Stonewater, but his explanation—that he was ill at ease at the castle with his host gone and needed time to work out a plan for his future—made sense, and Féolan was willing. However, he had blindfolded Derkh for the last two hours of their journey, explaining that he could not, without the council's permission, allow a Greffaire to know the location of the settlement. Derkh had nodded his understanding, but Gabrielle knew he felt the humiliation of it.

Derkh's eyes had gone round with wonder when the cloth was

removed and he first beheld the Elvish community. "I see what you mean," he had breathed to Gabrielle. "It is more different than I could have imagined." These past days he had been even quieter than in Chênier, but he seemed more relaxed. Maybe it was easier here, she thought, where his difference would be attributed simply to being Human.

The shocking thing Derkh had said to the head of council came again to her mind. Féolan had spoken long with Tilumar to explain their seemingly outrageous request to harbor a *Gref Orisé* soldier. Finally, Tilumar had asked to speak to Derkh himself.

"Gabrielle and Féolan have declared you a friend," he said. "Yet you are also of the land of our enemy. Why should I trust that you return their friendship?"

"Gabrielle saved my life," answered Derkh, as if that one fact explained everything. "Twice, she saved my life." Tilumar waited for him to go on. Derkh shrugged with impatience. "It is a debt more binding than any I know. I would die rather than betray her."

"It is fairly spoken," said Tilumar. "But what of Féolan? He did not save your life. Rather, as I hear, he has done you harm, even to the slaying of your own father."

Derkh, dark eyes flashing, had drawn his slight figure up with a dignity that seemed beyond his years. Suddenly, Gabrielle felt she looked at another Derkh: not the uncertain boy, but the warrior destined for high command. "Féolan has offered up his neck in redress for my father's death, and I have refused it. Why should I give up the easy opportunity, to seek a harder one? There is no ill will between us."

After the briefest hesitation, Féolan had translated. Tilumar, visibly taken aback, had looked with long appraisal at both of them.

"I deem you speak true," he said at last. "You are welcome to stay in Stonewater, under the protection of Féolan. Yet, for the time being, if he leaves, then you also must depart."

It had been some time before Gabrielle was able to question Féolan in private about those words. She could hardly believe what he had done. She still did not know whether to be appalled or impressed by his action.

Standing barefoot in front of the washbasin, Gabrielle twisted back her chestnut hair and splashed water on her face. Tonight was to be her official welcome. There would be feasting and the telling of her story and hundreds of introductions and singing into the night. She wished she had had time to learn more Elvish. Féolan had been teaching her, and she could now hear the distinct words and phrases in the liquid stream of sound. She understood more than a little, but she was far from being able to carry on even a rudimentary conversation. She would cram words into her head all day, she resolved, and learn at least a simple speech to express her gratitude.

As THE SKY overhead darkened to deepest indigo, the surrounding trees brightened with many sparkling lights. Their branches and the beams of the great gazebo were hung with lanterns, so that to Derkh it looked as though the stars themselves had joined in the celebration. Nor was that the greatest wonder of this night. Food he had never tasted, music he had never dreamed of, the flowing stream of a hundred conversations he couldn't understand. And the people! Who could have imagined such a people? Or whatever they are, he amended to himself. Everywhere he looked he saw bright eyes, shining hair, graceful gestures. Smooth, fair faces. His eyes sought out Gabrielle and found her deep in conversation with an obviously pregnant woman with a tumble of black curls. She's as pretty as any of them, he thought with an absurd sense of pride.

Something nagged at him, though, about all these lovely people. He scanned the crowd once more and snagged it: Where were the old ones? None here were gray or bent or wrinkled. A legend of his own people flashed into Derkh's mind—that long ago, people who had become a burden were taken far out on the plain and left to the wolves and snow. Nobody believed it now, but… Maybe they kill off the ugly ones too, he thought, and snorted with sudden laughter.

"Something funny?" It was Féolan, with more people to introduce. It was kind of him to include Derkh, but really Derkh was just as happy—and more comfortable—watching from the sidelines. He smiled and offered Féolan an embarrassed shrug.

"Derkh, my parents would like to meet you. They have heard the story of how you became friends with Gabrielle. This is my mother, Lunala, and my father, Shéovar."

Derkh stared at the two Elves standing before him. His parents? They didn't look one day older than Féolan himself. The woman, Lunala, touched her breast and held out her palm, and awkwardly he met her hand with his as Gabrielle had taught him.

"Welcome, Derkh," she said in Krylaise. "It was a difficult road, I understand, that brought you here. May you have a happier journey from now on."

That nearly undid him. This compassion from strangers—he would never get used to it. On such a dreamlike night he could almost believe happiness did wait for him, and he felt his resolve waver. He touched palms with Féolan's father, then excused himself for the food tables.

He wasn't alone there for long. Glancing up from his over-loaded plate, Derkh saw Féolan's friend, Danaïs, working his way across the gazebo. Derkh's first impression of Danaïs had been "an Elvish Tristan"—at least they both shared a light-hearted humor that was hard for even a stolid Greffaire to resist. Danaïs's daughter was one of a handful of children flit-ting about the party like pretty moths. Elf children, Derkh observed, didn't seem to have a bedtime.

"I must take Gabrielle sternly to task," Danaïs said by way of greeting. "It's obvious she has been starving you during your stay in Verdeau."

"Oh, no—," Derkh protested, recognizing just a hair too late that he was being teased.

Danaïs' soft brown eyes danced with amusement. "Eat up," he encouraged. "I don't doubt you are heading into a monu-mental growth spurt, and we will find you six inches taller by morning." He turned to more serious matters. "I came to offer myself as an imperfect translator. They are going to tell Gabrielle's story—how she was lost as a baby, and how she refound her mother's people—and it is a tale not to be missed. Unless you know it already?"

"No, I'd like to hear," Derkh said. "I accept your offer, with thanks."

The story was told by an auburn-haired woman of com-manding presence—"Gabrielle's great-aunt," Danaïs whis-pered—whose clear voice held the entire gathering spellbound. She told of a healer named Wyndra, who set off adventuring with her Human husband and new baby girl and was never heard from again. But Wyndra's child survived to have adven-tures of her own, and they had led her, through perilous and unlikely paths, back to her beginnings. When Gabrielle was finally called forward, laughing and crying at once, to be embraced by her great-aunt, the Elves burst into song. "It is the naming song we sing for infants," Danaïs told him afterward, his own eyes shiny with tears. "We sing it for her again, for this day she is adopted back among us. Come up now and wish her well."

And Derkh did, grateful for the chance to shake off his usual constraint and hug her tight. He had never known a goodbye so painful, unspoken though it was. But Gabrielle had been rejoined with her people. It was time—past time—for Derkh to rejoin his.

"At last a day that is ours to spend as we please. I am at your service." Féolan executed a perfect court bow and spoke now in Elvish: "Is there some wish in your heart you would follow?"

Gabrielle realized there was. She was shy to mention it—it seemed a foolish whim, set against the drama of war and death and love and healing they had been living—but it had whispered to her since the day she had first seen the relationship of Elves to animals.

"I don't know if..." She stopped, daunted by her own doubt: perhaps she would not be capable. Human and Elvish traits mixed in unpredictable ways, Orianne had said. She had been blessed with the gift of healing. There was no reason to expect there would be more.

"Tell me."

"Oh, Féolan, do you think you could teach me to talk to Cloud? Talk *with* her, I mean, like you do?"

He was laughing at her. "A day with her lover, and she wishes for the company of a horse!"

"You're right," she apologized, flustered. "I don't know what I—"

"Nay, my love," he waved away her embarrassment. "I am only teasing. I'm sure you can do it, and I would love to help you."

Soon Gabrielle found herself in the stables, standing in front of Cloud and feeling foolish.

"What do I say? Should it be in Elvish?"

"The words are not important," said Féolan, "though she will learn to recognize many words, in time. It is her mind, or maybe more truly her heart, you must speak to with your own. You need to send her the image, or feeling, of what you are saying."

Gabrielle stroked Cloud's nose, gathering her thoughts. What did she want to tell her horse? Cloud nuzzled at her, as if to say, Well, aren't you going to groom me or feed me or ride me? Gabrielle stepped close to Cloud's ear and whispered, "Cloud, thank you for our years together." Cloud's ear twitched at the tickly sensation, and that was all. Gabrielle gave a humiliated little laugh. "Féolan, I haven't the slightest idea how to do this."

"I think you do!" he insisted. "Gabrielle, forget the words. Maybe they get in your way. When you use your gift of healing, your mind touches your patient's body in some way, does it not?"

"Yes," said Gabrielle. Suddenly it was obvious. "Yes," she said, excited now.

"This must be similar. But instead of the body, you are touching another responsive, aware mind. That night we found each other after the raid, could you sense the comfort I tried to give you?"

"Yes."

"Not just from knowing how I felt about you, but directly from my heart to yours?"

"Yes, I felt it. From Danaïs once too." She noted Féolan's quizzical glance. "When you first left Verdeau. He helped me get through that awful goodbye," she explained. She hesitated, then added softly, "I felt I was about to break into pieces."

Féolan's finger traced the line of her cheekbone and grazed her lip. "The hardest thing I ever did was to leave you that day. But see, you already have the skills you need. You just need to direct them differently."

Gabrielle laid her head against Cloud's neck and twined her finger's in the horse's dark mane. She quieted her mind, focused in, and her awareness slipped into the powerful body. But now how to…? She remembered how she had once tried to reassure Justine's unborn baby. *Cloud?* Looking now not for injury or disease, but for a flicker of awareness, she gathered her affection for this gentle creature and sent it out.

A startled flash flared back at her, and she laughed with astonished excitement.

"Easy," cautioned Féolan. "Do not frighten her."

She tried again: *Cloud, it's me. It's all right.* This time warm recognition rushed back at her. From Cloud's generous heart she read love, and loyalty and submission, and this last pained her beyond words. *Friend,* she offered. *I would be your friend, not your master.*

Gabrielle's eyes were bright with tears when she opened them and spoke again to Féolan. "I didn't know," she murmured. Cloud's velvet charcoal muzzle whiffled her hair, and she laughed and stroked the horse's long nose. "So much I don't know."

"And so much you do," said Féolan. "It's amazing what you have already learned on your own." He smiled down at her. "You may be half-blind and clumsy as a toad, but there is nothing wrong with your mind."

"Nice. Insult the woman you claim to love." Now it was Féolan's turn to become penitent, until Gabrielle laughed and reminded him, "You deserved that."

"So I did." Féolan touched her shoulder, serious once more. "Gabrielle, why don't you ask Cloud if she would like to come for a ride with us?"

FÉOLAN PEERED OUT the doorway of the barn, scanning the path for Gabrielle. Still no sign. How long does it take to deliver a quick message? he thought, striving with limited success not to feel irritated by the wait. Gabrielle had left some time ago, just to change her clothes and tell Derkh they were going riding. He paced again to the back of the dim fragrant barn. Some of the horses shifted and champed as he passed—he was beginning to irritate them! Derkh might be still abed, he mused. It had been a very late night, and Humans seemed to feel the lack of sleep more than Elves. But no, surely Gabrielle would simply have left word.

He knew Gabrielle felt responsible for Derkh here, and he understood why. He just wished it wasn't so difficult to steal a little time alone with her.

A few minutes later Gabrielle hurried into the barn. One glance was enough to see that something was wrong.

"Gabi, what it is?"

"Derkh's gone."

Misunderstanding her anxiety, Féolan said, "I'm sure he's fine. He's probably just gone for a walk or a swim…" He broke off, interrupted by Gabrielle's impatient head shake.

"No, Féolan, he's really gone. I think he means not to come back." She held out a curl of birch bark. "He left this and all his Verdeau clothes folded in a pile."

Féolan unrolled the white bark and stared at the brief message, crudely carved into the surface: *GOOD-BYE.* And underneath that: *SORRY.*

Fear washed through him—could the boy mean to take his own life? Then he remembered how Derkh had lingered by the food table at last night's celebration, to the point that Danaïs had teased him for his bottomless stomach. He had been stashing food, Féolan now realized. Preparing for a journey, then, not death. In the wake of his relief came a deep regret. He knew where Derkh must be headed, and what awaited him there. It wasn't a life he would wish for a friend.

Gabrielle was fighting tears now. Féolan liked and cared for the quiet young man, but Gabrielle, he saw, had come to love him.

"We have to go after him," she said. "He can't just run off like this!"

Féolan was doubtful. He draped a comforting arm around Gabrielle's shoulders and tried to gather his thoughts. He understood the desire to follow Derkh, and since he had a good idea where the trail headed, there was a decent chance he could find it. But would Derkh thank them for it?

"Gabrielle," he offered. "Let's think a moment. If you meant what you said when you offered Derkh a home in Verdeau, then he is as free as anyone to go where he wishes, is that not so?"

"Yes, bu—," Gabrielle began, but he held up a finger to forestall her.

"And if he wishes to leave without long explanations and goodbyes, much as we might wish it otherwise, is it not his right to choose?"

"Yes, I suppose—but Féolan, why would he want to?"

He could no longer hide his dismay. "I think he has decided to go back to *Gref Oris*. That's why he left from here—less country to travel on his own. And if I had to guess, I'd say he felt he could never explain to you why he was going, or maybe he was afraid of losing his resolve. So he slipped away late last night, while we were distracted by your party."

"But why?" she blurted out. "If that place is as bad as you described, why would he go back?" He felt her unspoken question as a wave of hurt: *Could it have been so bad in my own home?*

"I don't know, Gabrielle," Féolan said softly. "Derkh's old life was very…defined. Maybe he didn't know how to make a new start."

Gabrielle pressed her hands to her eyes and took a deep slow breath, and Féolan felt her clamoring emotions become quieter. She stood that way for some time. "I don't mean to stop him," she said finally. "But I do want to say good-bye, if he's really bent on leaving. And does he even know where he's going? We could ride him to the border," she suggested.

"That's what worries me," confessed Féolan. "I expect he's a competent navigator in his own country. But he doesn't know the deep forest, and if he's making north for the mountains he's going through miles of wild terrain."

"You think he's in danger?" she asked.

"This land is dangerous for any but experienced woodsmen," he replied. "And what I saw of *Gref Oris* is mostly open plain. Yes, I think he could easily get himself lost, and I doubt he has more than a few days' worth of food. So I agree with you, after all. I'll have to go after him."

"We," she corrected.

"Gabrielle, I'll move faster without you. I really think—"

"We."

He took in the squared shoulders, the lifted chin, and sighed.

"Pack a blanket, a change of clothes, and wear good boots. Meet me at the kitchens. I'll have packs for both of us."

Her grateful smile lit up the barn.

"I won't hold you back."

CHAPTER SEVEN

DOMINIC leaned against the fence, his hands steadying Matthieu where he balanced on the top rail. Inside the ring, perched on her fat pinto pony, Madeleine tried to follow the riding master's instructions:

"Heels down, Mademoiselle! Always your heels down. Now, pretend you have no reins. Can you turn the horse toward me without them? Use your legs and knees to tell him where to go…"

Though Madeleine squeezed and nudged mightily with her thin legs, the pony walked stolidly on, straight ahead. Madeleine squealed in frustration, and Dominic hid his smile behind Matthieu's back.

"Dominic!"

Tristan loped across the field to the ring. A piece of parchment flapped in his hand.

"What is it, Tristan? You look… Have you had bad news?"

Tristan nodded. "From Rosie. Dominic, would you read this? I need your advice."

"You want me to read your love letter?"

"It's not… Look, just read it, okay?"

"Sure. Take Matthieu."

Rosalie's letter explained the tense look on Tristan's face:

Oh, Tristan,

We are in the most awful bind. Even now, it doesn't seem possible that this has happened.

That man I told you about who wished to marry me—his name is Pierre LaBarque. I didn't tell you before, but when I refused him he was very angry. It scared me in a way I can't quite explain.

Now he has come to Father and threatened to ruin him if we do not wed. The threat was carefully veiled and hidden, but he hinted at fires and other "accidents" and even our deaths.

I don't know what to do. I said we should go to the Regent's Guard, but Father says there is no witness and that LaBarque's words were so indirect that he could deny it and say he was misunderstood. But there was no misunderstanding his meaning. I am sure the man is dangerous—there is something so cold and calculating about him. We might hire guards for our house, or even move to the safety of Chênier, but he could still destroy our fields and warehouses or even harm the farmers who work our lands. Father says he is powerful enough to buy any kind of evil-doing.

Tristan, if there is anything you or your brother can do, please help us. I'm so frightened.

Your love, Rosalie

TRISTAN WATCHED DOMINIC'S mouth set in a grim line as he read. He forced himself to wait until his brother looked up from the letter, then asked, "Do you know this man?" Dominic had been in Chênier since before the war, having been left in charge of the protection of the royal city—and the queen—in the event

Greffaire forces broke through the main line of defense. But as regent of the south coast, he and his family lived in Blanchette.

"Oh, yes," Dominic replied. "Everyone on the coast knows LaBarque. I have thought more than once that his wealth grows beyond the pace of honest trading, but there has never been any evidence of crime attached to him. He is careful, as Rosalie says." He shook his head and muttered, "I've been away too long."

"Dominic, he must be stopped."

"Of course he must. One of us must go down there." Dominic eyed his younger brother. "I suppose it is of no use asking you to stay here for the joint defense meetings? I am the territorial regent, after all. This is my rightful concern."

"You're kidding, right? If some old maniac threatened Justine, would you head off to a meeting?"

"No. Not if I had a brother to send in my place," Dominic conceded. "But Tris, you will have to be very canny—you can't just charge in brandishing your sword. You should take a guard to protect the Martineau manor, though, and if you can possibly persuade André and Rosalie to come up here for the time being, it would be wise."

"So you agree with Rosie that the man is dangerous?"

"I do. He is ruthless and smart. When a man like that puts his own desire above all else…"

Dominic hoisted Matthieu off the fence and settled him onto his shoulders. "C'mon Matthieu, let's go find your grandmama. Your Uncle Tristan and I need to have—"

"I know, 'nother meeting." Matthieu brought his small fist down on his father's head like a gavel as he passed judgment: "Meetings, meetings, smelly old meetings!"

TRISTAN WAITED IN the spacious front hall while the maid announced him. The men of the Royal Guard who had accompanied him to the coast remained on duty outside the door. He had seen nothing amiss as they rode up the long lane to the Martineau manor, except perhaps a certain closed brooding look to the house itself—he had imagined that, no doubt. But there was no mistaking the way the maid's uneasy face flooded with relief when she recognized him.

"Tristan!" Rosalie appeared in a rush and flung herself around his neck. Tristan took his time with their greeting, holding her close, kissing her thoroughly and enjoying every minute of it. He saw no reason not to mix business and pleasure, if chance allowed. A measured tread on the stairs alerted them to André's arrival, and Tristan straightened up to greet his future father-in-law.

He was a little shocked at André's appearance. Drawn and stooped, André seemed to have aged a decade. It was the mark of fear; anger flared in Tristan against the man who had caused such a poisonous change.

Rosie would not sit in the parlor—"It reminds me of that odious man," she sniffed—so they ensconced themselves in André's study. Tristan listened carefully as first Rosalie, then André, recounted all they could remember of their dealings with LaBarque. He felt his face stiffen with disgust and outrage; never had he encountered such cold rapaciousness.

André's voice trailed off, and Tristan felt the man's cautious eyes upon him. "Tristan, I am grateful for your presence here. But I beg you to cool your blood. If you openly confront LaBarque, you could harm us as easily as help us."

"I do propose to pay the man a visit," Tristan confessed, seeing that it was time to unveil the plan he and Dominic had crafted.

"Not," he reassured, "to teach him a lesson with my sword, though I long to do so.

"No," he mused. "In fact, I don't believe we will speak of these matters at all. I am here, as a matter of fact, on official business. As future regent of Crow Island and the Blanchette coast,"—here Rosalie gave a gasp of surprise, and Tristan allowed himself to bask just for a second in her delighted pride—"I feel it my duty to make the acquaintance of the prominent personages and business interests in the region. Moreover, as the current regent will be required in the defense talks for some time to come, he has asked me, acting in his stead, to ensure that the governing of the region continues in good order."

It was true that Solange had proposed that the regency go to Tristan. Though more than capable of carrying the crown of Verdeau alone, she needed someone at her right hand, ready to step in if anything should happen to her. It made sense for that someone to be Dominic, the heir to the throne. Within the year then, barring another invasion, Dominic would move his family to Chênier and begin to acquire an intimate knowledge of the players, issues and duties of the royal court, while Tristan would take over the governance of the country's most important region.

The mood had changed in the little room. André sat straighter, his manner attentive now. Tristan flashed him a tight smile. "Baron LaBarque, I understand, is an influential and wealthy merchant. I am called upon to introduce myself, I think, and to discuss with him my plans for improving the area's prosperity. I will ask his advice on the troubling reports I have had of shady dealings, intimidation and outright crime among some of the merchants. I fear an intensive investigation may be required. He will be glad to hear, also, that although he missed the last call to arms it is not too late to support the country's defense efforts. We will need a continuing supply line for the forces posted at our borders, and while it goes without saying that a man of his wealth will want to contribute heavily toward our material needs, I think I might also be able to pull rank and secure him the honor of establishing and overseeing the transports himself. Surely he can spare the time away from his own thriving businesses to ensure the well-being of our troops."

André gazed at Tristan, as though for the first time. "I have underestimated you, I think," he said softly.

"Let's hope LaBarque has too," replied Tristan. "I am being a little flippant here, but this is a deadly serious game. I'll be honest, I'd be happier fighting him. But since he has not yet openly broken a law, we must turn his own methods against him. I expect he will recognize a veiled threat when he hears one."

Rosalie broke in. "It's nearly dinnertime. Do you want to put your things in your room and freshen up first?"

"I'm afraid I must stay at the regent's residence, at least for the moment," said Tristan. "This is to be a proper royal visit, after all. But dinner sounds good. Oh, and it being wartime still, I traveled with six guards. I wonder if four could be billeted here, as the castle is full of Dominic's people." Rosalie and André appeared confused at this request. "If you divide them into night and day shifts, they will only require two beds," he prompted them, "and they can make themselves useful by keeping an eye on things while they're here."

Rosalie sprang into action, bustling off to see the guards—and their horses—housed and fed. They would all sleep better with seasoned soldiers patrolling the grounds.

André pushed himself to his feet as well and opened a glass-
fronted cabinet tucked into the corner of the room. Returning
with glasses and a brandy bottle, he poured out the dark golden
liquid and offered a glass to Tristan. Tristan was relieved to see that
the older man, though still careworn and drawn, had regained his
usual firm manner. "Your plan is sound, Tristan," said André. "But
watch out for yourself, boy. Don't let down your guard."

"Yes," agreed Tristan. "Friendly visit or not, I believe I will go
in full dress uniform—sword and all."

THE NEXT AFTERNOON, Tristan followed LaBarque's house-
maid down a dark hallway, leaving his two guards posted at the
door. Like the meeting he had held this morning with the head
of Dominic's council, the escort was mainly for appearances. His
discussion with LaBarque would be private.

The woman led him past a series of dark oak doors, all closed,
and showed him into a room at the end of the narrow hall. Tristan
thanked her, but she merely ducked her head in return and scuttled
off. Now there is a woman who is anxious to be somewhere else,
Tristan thought. Afraid of her master, no doubt.

He entered the room, a library or study dominated by a massive,
heavily carved table. Behind the table sat a man of medium build
and sharp features. Tristan gazed at a face that might once have
been handsome, before the thin line of the mouth had hardened
into a look of perpetual displeasure, before the dark eyes had taken
on such glittering, hooded craftiness. The overall effect was of
barely contained malice, and Tristan wondered how André could
ever have been gulled by such a creature. Then LaBarque rose,
offering a bland smile along with his hand, and it was as though
the menace and hostility had never existed. He shows me his

fangs, thought Tristan, but just a glimpse. Just enough to threaten without seeming to. The man was an actor, and a good one.

"Come in, My Lord," said LaBarque smoothly. "So kind of you to honor me with your presence." Tristan considered the outstretched hand. It was a gesture used among friends and equals and more than a little presumptuous in LaBarque's case. Tristan hardly cared for such conventions, but there could be no doubt that LaBarque's familiarity was deliberate. Let it go, he thought. A power struggle now might derail the entire discussion. He strode forward to greet the man—and LaBarque's eyes shifted to the back of the room, his smile twisting into a snarl. Tristan's skin prickled with alarm. He whirled about, and though his sword was drawn by the time he faced the three men who had stepped from the shadowed corner behind the door, a sword would be of little use against the arrows now trained upon him.

"Shoot him," rasped LaBarque's voice. "Now!"

CHAPTER EIGHT

ERKH had never been so glad of the rising of the sun, though the morning warmth brought out a horde of buzzing, biting flies even worse than the mosquitoes that had tormented him all night. He hadn't realized how pitch-black the deep woods could be or how dense. Expecting the same light woodlands he had seen around Chênier, he had struggled instead through a treescape choked with deadfalls and scarred with rocky outcroppings.

Wanting to escape the sentries' notice, Derkh had avoided all paths out of the settlement when he left, planning simply to head north toward the foothills. An hour out of Stonewater, he had already lost all sense of direction, blundering through a land that seemed to pitch always at some violent angle, never running level. At first his own determination kept him from turning back. Soon, he didn't know where "back" was.

He stopped now, arming the sweat from his forehead, and looked around. Pointless, he thought. Can't see more than three paces in any direction in this ill-begotten swamp. He was surrounded by trees, mainly spruce and cedar, each with a circle of dead lower limbs thrust out like pike-poles. He had learned last night to walk with his arms held up to protect his head after catching one of these in the temple. Awkward, especially when he took a misstep and fell, but better than being blinded.

The trees glowered and pressed upon him. Never thought I'd miss those freezing plateau winds, he thought bleakly, picturing the sweeping vistas and open sky of his homeland.

Easing down on a log and rummaging in his pack for food, Derkh let his mind rest along with his body. The whispery voice of panic that had muttered to him in the dark was silent now. *Panic is fear run wild.* Col's powerful voice leapt into his head. *Kill it, or it will kill you.* His father had certainly given him many chances to learn to overcome fear, Derkh reflected. Maybe those bitter lessons would save his life, after all. He closed his eyes while he chewed, tried to believe Col's claim that a few moments' rest were as good as a night's sleep.

He knew what he had to do. He had to find a footpath—there must be some; after all, the Elves did travel this county—or at least a rivercourse, to follow. Otherwise he would never find his way anywhere.

He craned his neck, trying to sense the steepest slope. He wanted to get as high as he could, somewhere with a view so he could look for a break in the foliage that might indicate a passable route. It was a long shot, he knew. He might climb many weary slopes without ever finding what he sought. But it was his only shot, so he picked a direction, ignored the protests of his wrenched muscles and started climbing.

AT GABRIELLE'S INSISTENCE, Derkh had not been questioned about the Greffaire plans, but on the march home he had overheard Tristan speculating and offered one opinion. "I doubt they'll try again this season," he told Gabrielle. "That was our entire invasion force. They would have to empty the internal security service to rebuild an army that size quickly. They lost a lot of equipment too. I'd say if the emperor wants to continue the invasion, they'll have to recruit and outfit a whole new force."

"Your internal security service is the size of an army?" said Gabrielle, incredulous. She wondered if she had misunderstood Derkh's accented words.

"We have a lot of internal security," Derkh had replied flatly.

DERKH'S GUESS HAD been accurate, as far as it went. But he could not have predicted the true state of affairs in Greffier.

The total defeat of the Greffaire army was met with black rage by the emperor. No one could explain how such a disaster had occurred. Of the few soldiers who straggled back, starving and exhausted, some raved with wild tales of ghost attacks, arrows raining from the sky and fell warriors materializing from the very air. Those who talked sense acknowledged there were none but Human foes, but still seemed confused about the actual course of events. They could not explain, for example, how the buffering front lines of conscripts had melted away, leaving the professional soldiers to bear the brunt of the fighting.

Only one fact was clear to the emperor, and he seized upon it: Col had had the advantage, and he had lost it. He had not pursued the retreating army immediately, and thus had given them time to summon reinforcements. The former hero of Greffier was officially denounced, his entire family stripped of their positions and plunged into poverty. Thus did the emperor deflect blame from himself and his policy.

Nor would he accept defeat. Was he not emperor? To build an empire, there must be conquest. His advisors and nobles, as usual, voiced no objection to his plans to raise a new army, this time under a commander "who can execute a simple order." But some exchanged dark, cautious glances, and many more brooded alone over the emperor's latest excess. The invasion of Verdeau had been expensive indeed, and having financed the effort heavily from their own pockets, the nobility of Greffier were not anxious to refill both the royal coffers and the military barracks.

And where were the soldiers to come from? Men had already been pressed freely from the grain fields and cattle ranches that fed the country, and they had not been replaced. The harvest would be meager, the winter hard. Starving men, some muttered, make poor warriors. Before the snows had passed, the secret rumblings of alarm would flame into the first open rebellion in Greffier's known history. Civil war, not conquest, would occupy the Emperor's Guard come spring.

But that lay in the future. Now, the emperor demanded plans for a new offensive. His military tacticians and commanders—what was left of them—considered their options anxiously, and came to one cautious conclusion: they needed to know more about what had happened in Verdeau.

FOUR DAYS OUT from Stonewater, Gabrielle and Féolan were high in the Krylian foothills, well west of the Smoky River. They scanned the bare dry slope before them, looking in vain for some sign of Derkh's passage.

Derkh's journey through the forest had been easy enough to follow. With the help of a half dozen hunters and scouts recruited to check the outskirts of the settlement, they had quickly picked up his trail north from Stonewater. On the first day, even Gabrielle could spot the broken branches and scuffed loam—not to mention the odd dab of blood or "crash site"—that marked Derkh's painful nighttime travels. After that, Derkh must have traveled in daylight, for the trail became less blundering and more direct. Bewilderingly, it had led them straight up several steep hills and down again. Gabrielle had worried about this, picturing a panicky, irrational attempt to flee the forest. Then, after the fourth climb, the trail led them to a brook.

"Good thinking, lad," Féolan had murmured as they followed the watercourse northwest. "He learns fast, Gabrielle. He must have spotted the break in the trees from that last hill and made his way here. Now at least he won't wander in circles."

By the time the little brook joined up with the Smoky River, it had become a rushing highland stream, and the two travelers could look back and see miles of forest falling away like a green ocean behind them. They were on the shoulder of the mountains now, and the trees and underbrush had become sparse.

Derkh had followed the Smoky River north until he found a place where he could cross it. He then headed west—or as nearly west as the rocky outcroppings and steep gullies of the land allowed. Once away from the watercourse, though, his trail grew faint.

"He could have turned west sooner and saved us all some trouble," grumbled Féolan. "The traveling is easier in the lower foothills, and there's enough earth to take a footprint." The slope they stood on was peppered with rock shoulders and patches of loose scree, filled in with a dry tough grass that barely dented under their step.

Gabrielle scanned the horizon anxiously, as if she might actually catch sight of Derkh. "We must be close now, don't you think?"

"Maybe," said Féolan. "We lost time this afternoon, though— it's been slow going. And now…let's walk ahead a little and cast around on the far side there. But I'm afraid I may have lost him."

Gabrielle held her arms out against the stiff wind that gusted across the hillside as she squinted into the afternoon sun. She had never traveled the high country. The long vistas unfolding before her, the crisp clarity of the air, the looming sense of the mountains rising over them—all would have been exhilarating if she had not been so worried. She was tired too—though she would never admit it to Féolan. Needing to make the most of the daylight, they barely stopped from sunrise to sunset, and the terrain was much rougher than the south Basin woodlands she was used to.

He glanced back and stopped and waited while she drew even. "Cheer up," he urged. "Even if the trail is gone cold, we are not foxed yet." She looked a question. "He is making for the Skyway Pass," Féolan explained. "And I am no scout if I cannot get there faster than a lost…" He stopped abruptly.

"Did you hear that?"

Gabrielle nodded, eyes wide with alarm. The keening cry that floated in on the wind had stopped the breath in her throat—even in its faraway faintness it was savage with despair and pain.

They stood frozen, ears straining. Gabrielle knew enough not to interrupt the silence, though her mind swarmed with anxious questions. There, again—the hairs stood up on her arms at the sound of it. Gods of earth and sky, let that not be Derkh, she prayed. But who else would be roaming this wild country? No wolf or highland sheep had made such a cry. Gabrielle tried not to imagine the horror that might pull such an appalling sound from a young man.

Féolan was pointing just north of the prevailing wind, into the higher country. "Over there, I think." He was already leading the way.

CHAPTER NINE

I F the assassins had followed LaBarque's command immediately, Tristan would have been dead before he could even grasp the situation.

But they hesitated.

And Tristan, his reflexes still sharp from battle, seized the split-second of opportunity to act. He dove under the desk, toward LaBarque. He heard the twang of bowstrings, felt a stab of pain in his calf and another as he yanked his leg in under the desk. Tristan ploughed straight into LaBarque's chair—and there was his one chance. He grabbed the front legs and yanked them up. The heavy chair crashed to the ground, taking the startled LaBarque with it. Struggling through the crowded space, Tristan lunged at the fallen man. His head bloomed into red pain as it crashed into the thick overhanging lip of the desk, momentarily blinding him. LaBarque cursed viciously, and Tristan scrabbled after his voice while the blackness receded.

Fighting his way clear of the furniture proved more difficult than fighting LaBarque. The man had managed to pull a knife on his way down, and Tristan's sword was too long to manage in such a tight space. But LaBarque, though he knew his way around a blade, was no gutter-fighter, nor did he have Tristan's strength. Tristan grabbed at LaBarque's knife hand with both of his own and slammed it viciously against a chair leg—the weapon clattered to the floor. It was the work of a minute to haul the man to his feet with his own blade against his throat. Chest heaving, Tristan eyed his three assailants. They didn't look like soldiers or even criminals. They still held their bows, but uncertainly, aiming at nothing in particular. Their faces registered identical expressions of shock. It was clear they had no idea what to do.

"Curse you for idiots, all of you!" snarled LaBarque, and the three men seemed to shrink and bristle at once, like dogs that had been beaten. "You will pay beyond the powers of your feeble minds to imagine, that I promise you!"

"It's over, LaBarque," said Tristan quietly. Was it madness that drove this man beyond all reason? Tristan wondered if he even recognized his own defeat. "It will not be you doling out punishments hereafter. You are charged with the attempted murder of a prince of Verdeau."

"A lie," returned LaBarque promptly. "You have no witnesses. And I have my men here to testify that I was attacked in my own home without provocation, by a spoiled royal darling who doesn't want to share his toys."

Tristan was barely listening. He was watching the change that had just swept over the men. Two had drained of color so rapidly he thought they might faint or be sick. One, too florid to ever be pale, flared even redder, his eyes bulging in rage or terror. While the first two let their bows slip unheeded to the ground, this one hurled his against the wall with a curse and rushed forward.

Was the man going to attack with his bare hands? Tristan thought of his sword, dropped under the table in the struggle. He had the blade under his foot, but had not yet managed to pick it up. And his leg was hurt; he didn't yet know how badly, but he could feel the arrow hanging from his boot, stabbing into

flesh with every movement. Could he defend himself and keep
his hold on LaBarque?

As the man came around the table, Tristan swiveled to face
him, using LaBarque as a shield. But the charge stopped short as
suddenly as it had started.

"WHO ARE YOU?" the man shouted at him. It was the cry,
Tristan realized, that comes from urgency so great there is no time
for niceties. He overlooked the breach of etiquette and answered
simply.

"I am Tristan DesChênes of Verdeau and your liege lord."

The sandy-haired man in the corner groaned and sank his face
into his hands. But Red, as Tristan was beginning to think of him,
stepped up to LaBarque and spat square in his face.

"You told me we was to kill that murderin' foreign pirate captain, him that sank my son's ship! Not the son of our own king,
what died in the war!"

LaBarque sneered at the man's tirade. "Pirate, prince, what difference does it make? It's not like you had a choice, now is it?"
His words died into a gurgling grunt, as a large red fist smashed
into his mouth.

Take control, warned a voice in Tristan's head. Or you've lost
it for good.

"Return to the others now, sir," said Tristan, putting all the
confidence and command he had into that one phrase.

But the fight had gone out of Red. He turned to Tristan. "I'd
have fled the country, with my whole family too, before I would
knowingly 'ave hurt you, whatever his threats. May the dark gods
take me if that en't the truth." And he walked meekly to his companions and sank to his knees.

What to do with these men? The more Tristan observed them,

the more convinced he grew that they were neither conspirators nor thugs, but simple laborers who had somehow come under LaBarque's thumb: not blameless, certainly, but not guilty of treason either. To what purpose would he have them arrested? Yet, as LaBarque had pointed out, he needed their witness. If they bolted now, he would lose them.

"You, in the corner." He spoke to the tow-head, a very picture of despair. The man's head jerked up as though on a string.

"Me, Sir? My Lord? I mean, Sire?"

"You," he confirmed. "Help me here, will you?" Astonished, the man came forward.

"I need you to search this man. He may well be carrying a second knife. You are not to hurt him, but be thorough. You understand?" Pressing his own knife more firmly against LaBarque's skin, he murmured, "Arms in the air, My Lord. And not one threatening gesture, if you value your neck."

Tentatively, Sandy began patting down his employer, finding nothing on his initial search.

"Check his legs, especially inside his boots." Sure enough, Sandy discovered a second knife slipped into a pocket in the right-hand boot.

"Well done," said Tristan, as though he were addressing a soldier in his command. "Now see if you can find something—heavy parchment or cloth—to wrap both blades in, and stick them in my belt." Holding his breath, Tristan presented his back to a man who had been hired to kill him—and waited while the knives were gently tucked into place. It was a considered risk, to put the knife within their grasp—a demonstration of trust that, Tristan hoped, would align them on his side and against LaBarque. By the time it was done, the change in the room was palpable. The men were alert, their eyes trained upon him. They sensed they had been offered redemption and strained to grasp it.

"Now, you." He pointed to the last man, who had been almost completely silent. He came forward eagerly and bowed. "I need rope, something to tie the prisoner's hands." In moments, the curtain cord was fastened tightly around LaBarque's wrists. Now Tristan took time to glance at the arrow digging at his flesh. With relief he saw that the arrowhead had not even completely pierced his boot leather. At such a range, he might have been pinned to the floor, but his hasty dive had forced a hurried draw at an awkward angle, and he would have nothing worse than an angry surface injury. It was the work of a second to pull himself free.

"Isn't there something I can do, Sire?" It was Red, positively eager.

Now Tristan allowed himself a small smile. "I think you have done quite enough already, don't you?" The men exchanged glances, not daring to share the jest. Tristan relented. Red was his best hope for the last step. "Go to the front door, and tell the two guards posted there I have need of them. Tell them I have arrested LaBarque." Fear jumped back into Red's eyes, but Tristan held his gaze calmly.

A bitter laugh broke the spell. "You send the pig to fetch his own butcher!" crowed LaBarque. "Almost I begin to admire you, young princeling." His lip curled in disdain. "You credulous fools! Prison looms before you, and you not only lack the wits to run, you leap to the aid of your jailer. You, not I, have attempted murder in this room. I strongly suggest you finish the job before it's too late!"

"But I think you are mistaken, LaBarque," said Tristan. "I heard you order these men to shoot me, yet they came to my aid.

They have had, in fact, several opportunities to finish me off, and each has instead demonstrated his loyalty. That is a strange sort of murder, is it not?" He watched as Red wheeled and marched decisively through the door.

As LaBarque was frog-marched from his home under guard, Tristan, severe now, addressed his little trio. "I do not doubt you were misled about my identity, but the fact remains you were prepared to kill another man," he said. "Pirate or not, this is against the law of Verdeau." They could not meet his eyes, but Red stepped forward hesitantly.

"Sir… Sire. He threatened us. LaBarque, I mean. Our families, like."

"Aye." Tristan nodded. "I am not surprised to hear it. That is the way of men like him. But that is a kind of piracy too, and others must stand against it.

"Now LaBarque may name you as accomplices in his trial. And if he does, you will have to come forward and beg the mercy of the court. But for myself, I am content to have your witness to his crime. I want you to go with Normand there"—he gestured at the remaining guard—"and make your statements as to exactly what happened. He will write it down, to be presented as evidence. And then I suggest you leave by the back door, if there is one, and put a substantial distance between yourselves and this house."

As the men filed past him, Red bent onto one knee and touched his fingers to his brow. "If you ever come back here, you won't find stronger or more loyal supporters than us, My Lord. That's a promise."

Tristan regarded him. "You have seen, I think, what I am made of this day. One day there may be need for you to stand up and show what you are made of."

At last he was alone in the study. He sprawled into a chair, letting the tension of the last hour seep away, and chuckled to himself.

"You had better support me," he said aloud. "I just saved your arse."

CHAPTER TEN

THE Greffaire strike team sent into Verdeau had been given clear, if demanding, orders: Avoid discovery; if possible without detection, examine the battlefield and the last Greffaire camp for clues as to what had transpired; and, most important, capture a Verdeau soldier or two for interrogation. The ten men traveled the Skyway Pass until they neared the foothills. Then they left the trail and picked their way slowly through the wild country, circling east and then south toward the mouth of the pass, hoping to escape the notice of any sentry forces posted along the main route.

The ten men were among the toughest-minded, most seasoned, military professionals remaining in Greffier. Not one of them believed in spook soldiers or any other gutless attempt at an excuse for the Greffaire defeat. Even so, their first shadowed sight of the creature they inadvertently trapped in a blind gully had stunned them. Manlike but no man, hugely powerful, it burst roaring at them from the dark jumble of rock like a nightmare spun from the fevered accounts of the defeated Greffaire soldiers.

Later they were ashamed and never spoke of the wild, clamoring fear that gripped them in that moment—the harrowing visions of ambush and death at the hands of a hideous army. But four spears flew at the creature before they fled, and it did not pursue them.

When they had regrouped and realized there was no "army" but only a solitary foe, some of the men wanted to go back and finish it off. But their captain forbade it.

"This ain't a huntin' expedition," he said curtly. "We're to bring back soldiers, not trophies. Get movin'."

DERKH LAID OUT his remaining food: two wedges of old bread, hard now as biscuit, and a handful of dried apple slices. He didn't need to count the apple slices to know his chances of making it over the mountain were slim.

He had done the best he could with provisions, but opportunities had been few, and he had greatly underestimated the length of the journey. The map he had studied back in Verdeau had shown but a short gap between the Skyway and Otter Lake, which Gabrielle had pointed out as close to the Stonewater settlement. In the open plains of Greffier it would have been less than two days' march. He had had no idea how slow his progress would be through such dense wilderness.

He guessed he was close to the pass by now. With the trees thinned out and the sun visible, he was confident again of his direction. But neither of his options looked good. He could venture out of the hills into the rural lands on either side of the Skyway Road, and try to beg or steal some food—if he could get there without being challenged by the sentry guard and if he didn't end up arrested for theft or vagrancy. Or he could head over the mountains with an empty pack and hope to make it home before collapsing from hunger. A man can live a long time without food, his father had told him—many days if he has water. But could he make such a strenuous climb? Already his head ached and buzzed with fatigue and short rations. And if he came under attack…He heard again in his mind the eerie cries that had made his guts do a slow roll just a few hours ago and shivered.

Col's voice seemed to ring in his mind: *What mewling talk is this? You're a Greffaire soldier, man! You'll do what you have to do, or you're no son of mine!*

Derkh broke a chunk off one of the pieces of bread and packed away the rest. Then he shouldered his gear and plodded on, gnawing on the dry crust as he walked. His father was right. If he was going back to Greffier, he'd better start acting the part.

The sun was dipping low, and he was starting to watch for a sheltered place to make camp, when he heard a sound that froze him in his tracks. Voices. He must have stumbled into a sentry camp or scouting party. Scrambling for cover, Derkh flung himself over a lip of land that dipped into a shallow ditch, fringed with stringy shrubs, and strained his ears. For a long minute he heard nothing. Then the breeze gusted and with it came the unmistakable sound of men, louder now, voices raised as if in argument. There was a short burst of rough laughter, and the voices died down into silence.

Derkh flattened himself into the dust and stones, wondering what to do. The men were not gone, for though he heard no more talk, other noises came to him on the wind. Clanking—of weapons, or maybe cook pots. The scrape of loose scree underfoot. Caution and curiosity battled within him. Just before the last light failed, he decided to creep away out of earshot while he could still see to do so. He would head north and slightly east, hunker down for the night and in the morning cut above the sentries back to the pass. He stood cautiously and took his bearings.

A thud, a metallic crash, a roar of pain or rage and a hurled oath: "WHORESON BASTARD!"

Greffaire, Derkh thought dazedly. He spoke in Greffaire.

"WE'RE LOSING THE light, Gabrielle."

For two hours Féolan and Gabrielle had scrambled through the mountain terrain, following the intermittent cries. There had been none for a long time now—but their hope had faded even before that. Acoustics in the mountains were deceptive and straight routes nonexistent; it was like trying to track an echo.

Gabrielle wiped the sweat from her face and glared at the surrounding country, as if willing it to give up its secrets. Then she glared at Féolan, as though this fruitless hunt were his doing. With a groan, she threw herself on the stony ground and concentrated on catching her breath and easing the burning fatigue in her legs.

Féolan hunkered down too and passed her the waterskin. "We'd better find a place to spend the night while we can still see. Even if there was still something to follow, it would be too dangerous to keep going once the sun is down." The summer sky was bright yet, but the sun hung low over the peaks in the west. Once it fell behind the mountains, night would come swiftly.

Gabrielle raised herself on one elbow. "But what if it's Derkh?"

"If it is Derkh, we could walk right past him in the dark," replied Féolan. "And if it's not, every hour we spend at this search takes us farther from his path."

He was right. He was right, but it felt wrong. Throat tight, eyes prickling with tears, Gabrielle struggled against her own frustration and fear. Flipping onto her stomach, she lay against the rough grass, letting her heart slow, seeking the stillness that led to wisdom. She felt the strength of the mountain's great shoulder under her, the quiet thrusting of life in the grass and lichens and insects surrounding her. Yet the alarm in her heart did not fade; it grew clear and insistent as a ringing bell.

She sat up. "Derkh's in danger," she said. "I know he is."

Féolan had no answer. "We will keep looking tomorrow," he said. Tomorrow, they both knew, might be too late.

TEN MINUTES LATER they were climbing again, heading for a place where a wall of rock was scored and pitted with dark openings. "There should at least be a cave or fissure there where we can get out of the wind," suggested Féolan. Though the summer sun brought bright warm days, the mountain air was chilly at night. They passed and rejected several possibilities, where the cracks in the rock were too narrow or shallow for comfort. Then came a great break in the cliff-side, several paces wide. They peered into the crevice, already deeply shadowed at the far end.

"It may be sheltered from the wind, but it hardly looks cozy," offered Féolan doubtfully. "Let's look a little ways farther. We can return here at need."

Gabrielle picked her way across the yawning gap. Then, from deep within the passage, she heard a wheezing sigh—wind maybe, whistling through some narrow outlet. But the crunch of rock that accompanied it was no trick of the wind. Something was in there.

Gabrielle swallowed. Her heart raced, as she watched Féolan string his bow and nock in an arrow. Never before had she feared the wild creatures of the woods, but in this stark place, with nightfall on their heels, the danger was palpable. They listened. Nothing. Then—a grunt, breathy and labored. And a keening cry—soft now, soft and strangely tender, but unmistakably the voice they had been following. The hair lifted on Gabrielle's neck.

She had heard men grunt with the pain of injury, heard women grunt with the exertion of childbirth. She had never heard a cry like that.

Féolan looked a question. Eyes wide, Gabrielle nodded. They would go in. Féolan pointed to the sword sheathed at her side. Reluctantly, she drew it. He was right again. In a sudden attack, there would be no time to fumble with weapons. They crept in step by step, allowing their eyes to adjust to the deepening gloom.

The sounds came from the deepest recesses of the crevice, which curved as it penetrated the mountain. Cautiously, they eased around the bend. Gabrielle stiffened in shock.

Two large figures were revealed, indistinct against the rock wall. One lay, knees drawn up. The other crouched beside. The crouching figure rocked back and forth, keening softly. Gabrielle thought at first it was a huge man—but it wasn't. The creatures before her were furred, and they were larger than any man.

"Seskeesh," Féolan breathed beside her. He seemed almost transfixed with wonder. "I have heard of them. But never…"

Gabrielle, determined not to be more frightened than Féolan, stood her ground and stared. The prone figure let out a shallow grunting breath. Was it ill? Gabrielle looked at the creature carefully this time, through her healer's eyes. She noted the uneven heave of its chest, the awkward tilt of the head, the stiff limbs. It was suffering, she was sure of it.

Hardly aware of her actions, Gabrielle stepped forward. The crouching seskeesh's head snapped up, and in an instant it—she, Gabrielle saw—towered before them, roaring defiance. Eight feet tall at least, powerful beyond man or Elf, savage with fury, she was terrifying; yet Gabrielle was not frightened. Somehow she knew the creature would not leave her fallen companion to attack unless she had to.

"Féolan, don't shoot," she shouted. Could he hear in that awful din? Alertness radiated from him, humming like a bowstring. The creature—*seskeesh*, did he call it?—would have to be fast as lightning to reach her unharmed.

Slowly, deliberately, Gabrielle let her sword slip out of her grasp. She opened her empty hands wide and stepped a little closer. She took a deep breath, wondering if it would be one of her last. Unpracticed as she was, what hope had she really of reaching this alien mind? Yet she would try. She closed her eyes and stretched out her awareness.

It took only seconds. The *seskeesh*'s emotions blazed at her, fuelled by a fierce intelligence. Fear, grief, rage—they burned unveiled by any pretence, far easier to sense than a human's. It was her mate that lay dying. She would defend even his body with her last breath. Gabrielle groped for a way to make herself understood. She sent her own sorrow. She sent images of herself treating wounded men—but what would bandages and herbs mean to a wild creature? She imagined herself at the wounded *seskeesh*'s side, healing light flowing through her hands.

The *seskeesh* had quieted. Her attention was wholly on Gabrielle, and Gabrielle opened her eyes now and met the searching gaze of a pair of deep-set amber eyes. *Let me help*, Gabrielle pleaded silently. *Trust me.* Slowly the great shoulders lowered. Then the eyes snapped behind Gabrielle toward Féolan, still poised to shoot, and the fur seemed to bristle as a low rumbling filled the *seskeesh*'s throat.

"Féolan," said Gabrielle quietly. "I have to help her. I think it will be all right if you lay down your bow."

"She could break your neck with one swipe," he returned. "I can't protect you once you're working on him."

"I know," she said tightly. "Let's hope he doesn't die under my hands."

She heard Féolan's sigh, read into it all his worry, exasperation—and pride. "Healers," he muttered. She knew he had lowered his bow when the *seskeesh* settled back on her heels, watchful but no longer threatening. Gabrielle squared her shoulders and approached her new patient.

CHAPTER ELEVEN

In his darkest imaginings and fears, he had not foreseen this: to be cast as a traitor. Yet here he was, hands bound like a common criminal, blood dripping unattended from his nose. Hardly the welcome he had expected.

Derkh had known the true tale of his stay in Verdeau would be beyond belief in Greffier. He had planned instead to say he had been taken prisoner and then escaped. But he had not anticipated a hostile interrogation, so he had not worried overly about the details of his story as he approached his countrymen's camp.

"Prisoner, eh? And I suppose your clothes were piled neatly at the door, waiting for you?"

"I kept my clothes the whole time."

"Oh, aye. They must have had a nice washing and mending service for the prisoners of war. Three squares and complimentary haircuts too, I don't doubt." The burly soldier eyed Derkh with suspicion. "You're uncommon healthy-looking for a jailbird, boy."

Derkh remembered too well the one time he had accompanied Col to the military prisons: the filth, the prisoners' sores and matted hair, the smell, the constant coughing. It had been a place of utter misery. He tried a new tack.

Summoning to his mind his father's confident authority, Derkh stood straight, looking his interrogator directly in the eye. "Do you not wish to know who I am?" he asked quietly. "Captain, is it?" he added, noting the small pin on the right shoulder. Doubt entered the man's hard eyes. The young man had a compelling dignity for a scrawny coward-traitor.

"Well? Identify yourself."

"I am the eldest son of Commander Col, head of the Greffaire armed forces. I fought nearly to my own death at the first battle of the invasion, and if I am now treated with dishonor for returning to my own country, I assure you the displeasure of the High Command will be worse than any Verdeau prison."

The shock on their faces was gratifying, at least. Most of the soldiers snapped to attention and made to bow their heads. But the captain, better informed than his strike force, broke the tension with a derisive snigger.

"Col's son! Now here's a lad who's in for a sad surprise. I have news for you, boy. Your daddy's no longer the big cheese in Greffier. He's the man as botched the war, he is, and the Emperor's in a right rage against anyone whose name even rhymes with 'Col.' You'd do better not to go advertising your bloodline, you would."

Derkh could not hide his dismay. But as laughter swelled among the men, a hot anger rose in him.

"Is this how the emperor repays loyal service? My father laid down his life for the emperor's so-called glory. I would die rather than deny his blood." The truth of his own words came to him with a relief so deep it overrode, for a moment, his danger: he was not ashamed of his father, after all. He was not ashamed of himself.

"Ah, you'll have your chance soon enough, I'll warrant." The captain shrugged and turned away. "Keep him bound and watch him close," he ordered. "They'll want to question this one real thorough-like."

A tall balding soldier ambled over and shoved Derkh to the ground, tying his ankles together so that any kind of comfortable sleep was impossible. The man hawked and spat before speaking: "You'll be watched through the night, so lie quiet. Bother anyone's sleep and you'll pay—get it?"

Derkh got it, all right. He got that he had made a terrible mistake. There would be nothing for him in Greffier. Worse than nothing: humiliation and poverty at best, with death the more likely outcome. He had been a fool. Shivering in the biting mountain air, Derkh stared up at the stars and thought how strange it was that the Elves were so entranced with starlight. To him, they looked as bitter and cold as the bleakness in his own heart.

THROUGH THE LONG chill night Gabrielle worked, while Féolan and the great creature at her side kept vigil.

She didn't dare, at first, attempt anything that would cause pain to the fallen *seskeesh*. So she began with her mind, sinking into the concentration that washed away all fear and distraction. Three wounds there were altogether, the ugliest with the spear-point still embedded deep in the flesh. This she left—she could do little before the weapon was drawn. The long slash along his rib cage looked dramatic, but the strong bones beneath had prevented the spear from penetrating farther. It would heal on its own, if need be. Gabrielle's hands hovered over the neck wound. Small but gaping, it had formed a sticky pool of blood under her patient. And still it bled. In her mind's eye she saw the torn blood vessels, felt the powerful throb of a huge heart pumping the creature's blood out onto the rocks. Almost miraculous, it was, that the two great blood vessels bonemenders called the "heart paths" had been missed. She bent her head and felt the warm light flood into the wound through her hands. She sent it to ripped veins and arteries, surrounding them with light, and clamped down with her mind to seal the frail walls together.

For two hours, man and beast watched and saw nothing. The fallen *seskeesh* lay in uneasy sleep. The wound, outwardly, remained unchanged, for Gabrielle worked deep in the tissues where the true danger lay. Bleeding controlled, she searched for the dark particles that signaled dirt or infection, making of the light a barrier against them. Under her hands, damaged flesh began to regenerate and rejoin, becoming whole again.

Now she paused, considering. The spear must be pulled. She could feel the flesh around its point starting to fester. But though the female *seskeesh* seemed confident now that Gabrielle and Féolan meant no harm, she did not yet trust in Gabrielle's skill. She needed to *see* some improvement in her mate before she could allow Gabrielle to do what must be done. And so Gabrielle worked on, an hour more, hoping her patient's innate strength would keep infection from the spear at bay. She worked until the neck wound was no more than a shallow nick, and then she opened her eyes to the world.

It was fully dark now. The moon, nearly full in a clear sky, would be a bright beacon over the earth, but it was not high enough to penetrate their sheltered corner. Gabrielle sensed, rather than saw, the four eyes trained upon her, alert and protective. His mate and my mate, she thought. We are not so different after all.

"I need water now, and light, and a fire before I freeze solid," she said to Féolan. The night had seeped right into her bones while she worked. He looked doubtful. "Water and light I can do," he said. Slowly, so as not to alarm their companion, he rose to his feet and shrugged out of his pack, then unhooked the water skin.

"Is it enough?" he asked, handing it to Gabrielle.

"For now," she replied. "Oh, and I guess one of our blankets will have to go." The *seskeesh* tensed as Féolan drew his knife, but allowed them to cut the blanket into quarters unhindered. Gabrielle trickled water from the skin onto one piece, and rinsed the bloody, matted neck fur around the wound. "Now the candles," she murmured.

Féolan had just finished fitting the two stubby travel candles into their copper holder. She heard the scratch of the striker and felt the *seskeesh* start. As the tiny flame caught hold, the big female barked in alarm and drew up on her haunches. Afraid of fire, realized Gabrielle. She reached out a reassuring hand, encountered coarse hair covering a limb like a tree trunk.

"Put it out!" In a single moment of panic, Féolan could be killed. Gabrielle waited until she felt the great muscles ease and sink back, and then sent her thoughts out through her fingers. Images of harmless light—moonlight, sunlight—and above all the need to see her patient's injuries. She had no doubt the creature's night vision was better than hers, better even than Féolan's, but she wanted a really clear view. *No harm, no hurt,* she promised. How under the stars could such things be conveyed, without words? It took long, precious minutes, but at last Gabrielle felt it safe for Féolan to try again. This time, though the *seskeesh* bristled under Gabrielle's hand, she allowed Féolan to approach with the little lamp. When the small pool of light fell directly on her patient's wound, Gabrielle drew back, and gestured for the *seskeesh* to look.

The creature's amazed delight touched her deeply, but there was no time to bask.

"Féolan, that spear must be drawn," she murmured.

His troubled eyes, dark in the wavering candlelight, met hers. "I know it," he replied. "It's been on my mind this past hour."

DERKH WAS CATAPULTED from a thin sleep, heart pounding as though it would burst. Eyes wide in the inky blackness, he struggled to grasp what had wakened him. All around him men cursed and leapt to their feet, but the inhuman roar that had rent the night had already faded away. The dark silence covered it, and it was as though it had never been.

For long moments they strained their ears against the dark. Silence. Their leader slumped back to his blankets. "It's that ill-whelped monster," he snarled. "I bloody hope those were its death throes. It sounds like the very Hound of Hell."

Derkh pulled himself into a ball and tucked his hands between his knees in a useless attempt to generate some heat. The constant shivering was making his bound limbs cramp painfully. The Hound of Hell might be a welcome change, he thought. Though the dawn would bring warmth, it was unlikely to bring relief.

IT WAS THE fire, not the spear, the *seskeesh* could not accept. As soon as Féolan had moved the lamp to reveal the broken shaft protruding from her mate's body, it was clear she understood. Indeed she made to grab hold of the shaft herself, and Gabrielle had to intervene quickly to stop her from pulling on it. Gently Gabrielle laid her hand over the powerful fingers, marveling at the tough smoothness of the leathery undersides, and reached out with her mind. She showed the *seskeesh* how deep the spear had thrust, the heavy bleeding that was sure to come when it was removed. She painted the image of her fear: that the injured one, roused by the sudden fierce pain, would lash out unknowing and kill her. Last, Gabrielle showed her how it must be done: Féolan to draw the weapon, Gabrielle to control the bleeding and the *seskeesh* herself to restrain her mate and reassure him.

And so it was done. And though the great creature's maddened roar of pain as the notched blade bit against him left them weak with fear, though he bucked and writhed against the weight as Féolan pressed the wadded blanket against the gushing blood, still his mate held him and crooned to him, until at last he lay still.

Working feverishly to stem the tide of blood, Gabrielle was only dimly aware that her motionless body shook now with cold. She did not see Féolan lay out the firewood or the *seskeesh*'s tense attention on his flint, his patient attempts to explain the need or her final panicky scattering of his wood. What she did feel was the female's sudden presence looming behind her, the strong enveloping musk of her animal scent. Slowly the great creature lowered herself behind Gabrielle, pressed her great soft belly against Gabrielle's back, wrapped her shaggy arms about Gabrielle's shoulders and chest. Heat bloomed against her. Gabrielle sighed, leaned back into a wall of warmth, and sank deeper into the healing trance.

CHAPTER TWELVE

TRISTAN lounged back in the leather chair. LaBarque's claret was doing an admirable job of calming the jittery weakness that had washed through his legs in the aftermath of the assassination attempt. Gods of the deep places, he had nearly been killed by his own countrymen! He expelled a shaky breath and helped himself to another long swallow. Better.

Easy, he warned himself. Don't want to be pie-eyed when they come to hear your charges. Not relishing a visit to the lockup cheek-by-jowl with LaBarque, Tristan had instructed his guard to send the law clerks to hear him right on the premises. He straightened up at the sound of hurried footsteps in the hall. That was fast, he thought. But instead of the liveried clerks he expected, Red barged through the door, followed closely by Normand.

"You again! I thought I told you to clear off."

The man fell extravagantly to his knees. "M' Lord. Sire. Forgive me. I only just thought of it. I should've said earlier but it fair slipped my mind and…"

"What?" demanded Tristan, alert now. "Just say it, man!"

"Us three. We weren't the only ones."

"The only ones what?"

"You know, men as was hired by LaBarque. There was three others as he was talkin' to when we arrived. I seen him give them money, and he said, 'Your full payment when the job's done.'"

"What job?" snapped Tristan.

"I don't know, Sir. He never said. But Sir—Sire—those men weren't local lads like us, Sir. Rough-lookin', they was. I never seen them in these parts before, and they didn't seem, you know, like they were afeared of him. The one fellow, he says, 'In gold, mind—and the ship waiting as we agreed.' All business, like... Sire?"

With a startled shout, Tristan was on his feet and flying out the door. He cursed as he fumbled to untie his horse's reins—cursed the knot, cursed LaBarque, cursed his own stupidity.

Then he was galloping down the road, not waiting for Normand to catch up.

Rosie. Those men were going after Rosie.

THREE MEN, HEAVILY armed, lay hidden in the strip of brush kept as a windbreak along the far side of the horse pasture. For the past hour they had observed the Martineau property from every angle. Now their leader, the man known to them as Shade, was ready to lay his plans.

"So. The two guards we weren't expecting, but they won't hold us back any." His sharp eyes flickered from one face to another. His colleagues, as it amused him to call them, were nodding in cool agreement. He had expected no less. They had all handled tougher jobs than this.

"Aye, but Boss," objected Thorn. It was a precaution Shade insisted on: nicknames only. Thorn and Wolf were both solid professionals, but Thorn was the faster thinker. "Those're King's Men, them guards. LaBarque didn't say nothin' about Royal Guards, and more's the point, our fee don't say nothin' about them, neither."

"True enough," Shade agreed. As he talked, his watchful eyes scanned a circuit from the guard at the back door of the manor, to the barn, and across the nearby lawns and pasturage. "If LaBarque wants his girlie, he'll have to pony up a little extra for our trouble. If he doesn't—well, she's a pretty little thing, and we have his ship. She'll bring a high price in the Tarzine slave auction."

The men smirked, but they knew better than to laugh out loud. Nothing interfered with business when you worked with Shade. He got back to business now.

"There's no cover at the front entrance—just that wide driveway and low gardens. So we go in by the back. Thorn, you will distract our friend over there." A finger flicked toward the guard.

"You gonna tell me how?" Thorn asked.

"Fire. You can make your way to the barn right along this hedgerow. An unfortunate thing, when a barn catches fire. Disastrous, if people don't drop everything to help. Stick him in the confusion, if you can do it unobserved.

"Wolf, you and I go in the back. We head straight through to the front door, open it and take the guard before he realizes he has visitors. Then the girl. We meet up here, work our way back to where we left the horses."

Two curt nods were his only answer. Crouched low, Thorn moved into the underbrush. Shade and his silent colleague waited.

ROSALIE WAS TIRED, all right. She hadn't slept well in days, but it didn't take her long to realize that she wasn't about to sleep now, either. André's suggestion that with a guard on each door they could enjoy an afternoon nap was sensible, but how could she relax knowing that Tristan might be face to face with LaBarque at this very moment? Rosalie flopped over onto her back, pulled the quilt over her face to block out the light slanting through the open window and made a last effort to stop her mental hand-wringing.

Tristan would be regent. There was a thought worth savoring. Chênier and life in the big castle were, she supposed, more exciting, but to Rosalie a city without a seascape would always seem lacking. She would marry Tris, and they would live on her beloved coast. With LaBarque as your neighbor? The words came unbidden to her mind—and she was back to worrying again.

Enough! With an impatient sigh, she slid out of bed and reached for the dress she had hung from the bedpost. Her hand stopped midair, its task suddenly forgotten. Someone was shouting. Just one of the field-hands, maybe, but it sounded urgent. Rosalie was on her way to the window when she smelled the tang of smoke drifting in on the breeze. Fear rose in her throat. Just a grass-burn, she thought. Please let it be a grass-burn.

It was the barn. Black smoke rose from the far end of the building. As she watched, men ran from the nearby fields to help; Tristan's guard was already at the well, pumping water. Réjean, the groom, emerged from the barn, struggling with a pair of frightened horses. On his heels came a shrill scream from an animal still trapped inside. "Pray heaven, save the horses!" Rosalie whispered. She had the dress over her head in seconds, was reaching for her boots when she heard the other noise and froze.

Footsteps. Quiet slow footsteps in the downstairs hall. Not the busy trip of the maid. Certainly not one of the men bursting in to warn of fire. Rosalie had a sudden vision of the guard at the pump—the guard away from his post—and was sure. They had trouble.

For a second the blood pounded in her head so wildly the room swam around her. "Don't you dare!" her own angry voice slapped at her. She took a deep breath, forced her eyes to focus. Another breath. Now think. Leaving her feet bare, she padded silently across the room to the hook where her archery equipment hung. She eased the quiver across her back, strung the bow, fitted an arrow into place. Her own practiced movements steadied her. She was not helpless, not by a long shot.

Rosalie was creeping into the hallway, thinking about sneaking down the servants' stairway to the kitchen and how silly she would look if there was no intruder after all, when she heard the front door open. The rest happened in a blur: a man's voice, confused scuffling, a shocked cry of pain. It should have sent her down the back stairs in a hurry; but instead she found herself crouched at the front banister, peering down to the foyer.

Two men dragged the guard through the doorway and to one side of the wide entrance hall. A dark trail of blood followed them across the stone tiles. The man carrying the guard's ankles laid them down gently, and with a lithe, almost elegant movement, reached back with his foot and eased the door shut. He glanced down the long hallway leading to the back of the house. "Now for the girl," he said softly, drawing his knife and gliding across the foyer toward the stairs. He motioned his companion to stand guard by the door, then swept his gaze up to the stair landing. Rosalie stood at the top of the stairs, her bow trained on his heart.

CHAPTER THIRTEEN

THE chunk of dark hard bread Derkh was given for breakfast brought back a world of memories. "Soldier's bane," they called it, and Derkh had eaten it on journeys and in training camps for as long as he could remember. The taste was bitter to him now, the taste of a life lost. He ate it anyway, tasting blood with the bread as his split lip reopened.

And though he kept his eyes down, he listened while he ate. For reasons he couldn't fathom, he had not yet lost interest in his own fate.

"So what's next, Cap'n?" asked one of the men. "Do we take this'n"—thrusting his chin toward Derkh—"and head back?"

"You wish," grunted the captain—Tarkhet, Derkh had overheard the men call him. "Our job's to bring back one o' *their* soldiers, not our own! This lad's just gravy."

So that's what they're doing here, thought Derkh. But why? He tried to think like his father. To what end would an enemy soldier be useful? Information, obviously. That suggested a second invasion was in the wind. But something didn't add up. The information an invading force would need—numbers, deployment, defense plans—you couldn't just snatch some outpost soldier on lookout duty and expect him to know these things. And no one from Greffier, where only the highest rungs of the military were privy to big-picture plans, would assume otherwise. So then what…

His speculation was cut off by the next remark. "He'll be a right burr in the butt, that one, though, won't he? I mean, how quiet's he gonna keep while we go sneakin' up on his new friends?"

"The thought had occurred to me." Tarkhet's voice, dry, speculative. Derkh glanced through the dark tangle of his hair, to find Tarkhet's cold gaze leveled at him. He means to kill me, Derkh realized. He dropped his head, as though he could escape Tarkhet's notice by ducking under his sightline. The blood boomed in his ears and behind his eyes; he fought to keep his breathing normal and listen.

"Interrogation's not really my line," Tarkhet continued in the same flat tone. "But on a special mission you sometimes have to go a little beyond yer usual line." Tarkhet hauled himself to his feet and walked heavily over to where Derkh sat, his legs and hands still bound. The heavy boots came to a halt before him; Derkh looked up the broad trunk to meet pale eyes that betrayed no flicker of emotion.

"We'll question him here. If he convinces me he's loyal to the Empire, and is still fit to travel, we'll gag him and bring him along. If not," he shrugged, "you know what they say about dead men."

In the silence that followed, one of the men scratched his head and ventured a question. "Uh, what do they say about dead men, Cap'n?"

Tarkhet's humorless smile was a brief baring of teeth, nothing more. "They don't itch yer butt."

FÉOLAN PUSHED BACK the hood of his cloak and stretched

out his legs. How long would Gabrielle continue? The sky had brightened with dawn some time ago, though only now were the sun's fingers of light able to penetrate their shadowed nook from above. Both the *seskeesh* appeared to be asleep, the female snoring in Gabrielle's ear. How it had alarmed him when she first lumbered over there. Not that he thought she intended harm, not by then—rather he had feared some blundering, unintended injury. But no, the female had seated herself on the ground and arranged her huge limbs around Gabrielle with a surprising gentleness. And Gabrielle had hardly roused, just accepted the great beast's protection.

The experience had filled Féolan with awe, and he would have been in no rush to cut it short if not for Derkh. Two hours of daylight wasted already, and the trail gone cold to begin with. In any case, Gabrielle would be exhausted from her night's work. She would have to rest, and then they would have to make straight for the pass and hope to get there first. For the first time since they set out, it seemed a slim hope.

The *seskeesh's* rumbling sighs cut off as she started awake. Gabrielle stirred as well. She stretched, wincing as she straightened her head, and raising a hand up to rub her neck before her eyes opened. She gazed at Féolan with that slightly blurry look he had come to recognize as the lingering remains of her trance—as though the world was not quite in focus. He couldn't resist waving a hand.

"Over here, Sharp Eyes," he teased in Elvish.

"I see you. You had better have some food at hand, or I'll eat you alive."

The green eyes were clear now, the smile tired but untroubled. She was satisfied, then, with her night's labor.

Gabrielle squirmed around, laid a hand on the female *seskeesh*'s chest and murmured a few words. A thank-you, Féolan guessed, or perhaps detailed patient care instructions. He wouldn't put it past her—her powers of communication, untrained as she was, were stunning. Untaught rather: she had trained herself to heal and evidently acquired other skills in the process. For a moment he was overcome by his feelings for her: his admiration, his desire. His father's words came back to him and he sighed. When they got back to Stonewater, he would have to talk to her. He would rather be flayed alive than postpone their wedding, but he would urge her to do just that nonetheless.

"What's wrong?" Gabrielle's quizzical eyes upon him.

"Nothing. Just lost in the stream…"

"You were glowering as though you were lost in a pit of vipers."

Féolan shook his head and offered what he hoped was a distracting smile. Not now. "How's your patient?"

Now it was Gabrielle's smile that was distracting. She was beaming. "I'm sure he's out of danger. Once the repairs got started, and he got some strength back, it went amazingly fast. These creatures, Féolan, they are so…," she groped for a word, "vital. I've never encountered anyone with such a strong life-force…"

Her words faded as she came back to reality. "Derkh's even farther away now, isn't he?"

Féolan gave a reluctant nod. "Only a few hours, I guess, and we had lost the trail anyway. If we make good time to the pass and hit it far enough to the north, we still have a chance of intercepting him."

"Then let's go." Gabrielle got stiffly to her feet, making a visible effort to thrust away fatigue.

"Nay, Gabrielle. You will eat first and rest." Féolan held up a hand to forestall her objection and spoke with quiet conviction. "We cannot overtake Derkh if I have to carry you over the mountains. Come and take some food."

CHAPTER FOURTEEN

"TAKE one more step, Sir, and I will kill you where you stand." Rosalie had meant to sound commanding and confident, but the mortifying tremble in her voice betrayed her.

Tremble or not, the sight of her stopped the intruder in his tracks. For a second, shock and uncertainty played over his smooth features. Then, as he took in the silence of the second-floor hallway stretching behind Rosalie, the absence of any guards or companions rushing protectively to her aid, his face relaxed into a dismissive grin. "Good day, Mam'selle," he replied with exaggerated courtliness. "I am afraid this is not a good time for archery lessons. You are to come with us."

When the seas burn! thought Rosalie. Her voice might be wobbly, but her hands were steady. Steady enough. How steady did you have to be to hit a target straight on at ten paces? Just think of it as a target, she told herself. He has already killed at least once.

The man was muttering to his accomplice. Rosalie understood from their quick glance down the hall that he was sending the man to the back stairway. They would have seen it on the way in, she realized with consternation. He was out of her sight before she could gather her thoughts to act. Could she rouse the sleeping guards before she was sandwiched between the two men? You will have to shoot one of them—or both, she told herself sternly, though her mind recoiled from the coldness of it.

She kept her bow trained on the first man—the head, apparently, of whatever was going on here—holding him at bay, while her ears strained after the second intruder's progress toward the back stairs. If she shot the one in the hallway the second he came into view, could she have the boss back in her sights before he reached her? She would do better, she knew, to shoot the one she had now, but she could not bring herself to hit a motionless man. She edged back a little into the hall.

He was talking to her, but she tried only to listen to the approaching footsteps. "There is no need for you to be hurt, Mam'selle. Simply put down the bow and come along with my colleague."

Suddenly the back stairs thundered with running feet—he was coming for her, fast. Rosalie whirled about. The man was already charging down the hall at shocking speed. If she did not shoot now, he would have her. The bow twanged, and he fell, an arrow sprouting from his right shoulder. The sight of such a thing, in her own house, by her own hand, was paralyzing—yet she must move and now. Wrenching her eyes from the blood, pulling a fresh arrow from her quiver, she turned back to find the leader more than halfway to the top landing. She took two quick steps away, but could go no farther without losing her bead on his chest.

Once again they were at a standoff. Rosalie was light-headed with fear and shock, felt her arms tremble with it as she drew back the string. No doubt her assailant saw it too, for his elegant face regained its confident smile, and he dipped his head in mock admiration. His voice, however, was hard and commanding. "A lucky shot. I congratulate you. Yet it is time to stop this charade. You are outnumbered—the rest of my men are outside, awaiting my call, and you, young miss, are alone." Behind her, Rosalie heard furtive movement from the wounded man, the sound of a knife eased from its sheath. I should have killed him, she thought. He'll throw the knife, and that will end it. Pray heaven he is not left-handed.

A slight movement yanked her jittery attention away from her opponents. Rosalie watched, aghast, as the front door eased open. Not more! she thought, desperation rising to drown out her courage. I cannot hold off more of them.

The leader's grin broadened as he saw Rosalie's face stiffen in dismay. "You see. It is better you come now, before I must use my knife. You cannot hope to shoot us all."

"She can definitely shoot you, though," said Tristan affably. He had slipped through the unlatched door and was nearly to the first stair. Now the trap was reversed, the would-be captor caught between a bow and an advancing sword tip. Even as he turned, he raised his knife-arm for the throw.

"Try it, if you wish to die." Tristan's voice rapped out, hard and arresting. "Rosalie can bull's-eye a straw man at fifty paces. I'd put you at less than five."

For a long moment the man considered Tristan's words. Then, with a grunt that sounded more vexed than afraid, he glanced back at Rosalie. This time the bold eyes took in her neat stance, the relaxed three-fingered draw. With an ironic smile, he lowered his arm, turned his knife and presented its hilt to Tristan. "Well played. I concede." A second later, Normand barreled in.

A door clicked open behind her, and Rosie's heart surged. Then André's voice floated down the hallway, bleary with sleep.

"Rosalie? I heard voices. Is Tristan back?"

Dizzy with relief, Rosalie surveyed the scene below. Tristan looked so calm, but his blue eyes blazed at her. Cornflowers on fire, she thought. He can make a girl weak in the knees at fifty paces. Her own silliness made her laugh out loud.

"Yes, Father," she replied. Her voice her own again, thank heavens. "Tristan is back."

AN AGE CRAWLED by, it seemed, before Tristan was able to entrust the prisoners to Normand's care and bound up the stairs to Rosie's side. The off-duty guards had to be rousted out—incredulous, he was, at Rosalie's sheepish admission that she had put them in the old servants' quarters in the attic so they would be "less disturbed" by the noise of the household—the situation at the barn checked out, the grounds searched. The back-door guard, he was gratified to learn, had not been so easily duped, after all. Becoming suspicious about the source of the fire, he had left the water pump to other willing hands and investigated behind the barn. The night guards found him tying Thorn to the hitching post in the yard, both men coughing and red-eyed after a cat-and-mouse game through the smoke-filled building.

At long last Tristan and Rosalie sat together at the top of the stairs, arms twined about each other. She was perilously close to tears, he knew, but she would hold them back until the last stranger was out of her home. Now, as the dead guard's body was carried outside, Tristan held her head against his chest and kissed her hair. He had been a good man, Brousseaux, conscientious and steady. Tristan thought of the man's young wife—only a year wed, they were, with a baby on the way—and anger swelled in his heart that this man should escape the perils of war only to die under a countryman's sword. How many other lives, he wondered, had LaBarque ruined over the years?

Dinner was delayed that night. The cook and maid had rushed

with everyone else to fight the fire. When they came back, they were so unsettled to learn what had happened that it was some time before they could stop fluttering and exclaiming and begin cooking.

Tristan, Rosalie and André retreated to the parlor to wait. Rosalie and Tristan seemed unable to let go of each other, sitting nearly in each other's laps on the sofa across from André's easy chair as each recounted what had happened. Tea, and then tea with brandy, was brought in, and the bracing glow of it was so welcome that if not for the lurking fear of some new trap that might yet be sprung, they would all three gladly have drunk themselves silly. They were still piecing together the full extent of LaBarque's malignancy when the bell called them to table.

"Come back with me to Chênier," Tristan urged as they made their way to the dining room, "both of you. A little holiday will do you good after all this trouble, and frankly, I'd feel better knowing you were safe."

"It sounds like you were in greater danger than anyone, today," observed André. He looked at his daughter, her chair pressed tight against Tristan's, and favored her with an uncharacteristically broad smile. "However, I'm afraid it would take a bonemender's blade to separate Rosalie from you right now. And you're right, we could both use a change of scene. Give me a couple of days to put things in order here, and I will gladly accept your offer."

Tristan nodded with satisfaction. "That's settled, then. And you should sleep at Dominic's in the meantime, just in case. Unless you have some objection?" He nudged Rosalie in the ribs.

"No objection," she confirmed sedately. But her eyes danced, and she blew a kiss of gratitude to her father.

CHAPTER FIFTEEN

DERKH groaned as another heavy blow sank into his stomach. His body convulsed, trying to double over despite the bonds that held him upright against a tree. He had been here all morning, left to stand hungry and immobile while the men went about their business. That was bad enough. The interrogation, which had begun after the midday meal, was much worse. For the last hour, maybe two, he had been giving the same answers to the same questions, and Tarkhet's patience was wearing thin.

"Very soon now I will decide it doesn't matter whether you are left able to walk, and begin breaking bones. I advise you to think *harder* this time. Start again with the first battle."

Derkh spat blood. Somehow the fact that he hadn't the strength to clear it past his own chin seemed worse than the pain he endured. He felt sick with humiliation as the slimy mess dribbled down his neck. He no longer cared if they found him "loyal to the Empire." He had resolved, at the beginning of this ordeal, on just one thing: to keep the Elves and Gabrielle out of it. Not that they would believe either story anyway. He made an effort to pull his thoughts together.

"We won the first battle, as you know. Not easily, though. They were waiting for us. Somehow they knew we were coming."

"How many of them?"

"Far fewer than us. Maybe three thousand."

"Then why were they not pursued?"

"I don't know. I told you already, I don't know." Derkh braced himself for another blow, but it didn't come. "I was injured by then, half-dead. I showed you the scar. All I know is we stayed in our camp."

"For how long?"

"I'm not sure. I was fevered. Not long, I don't think. Then the camp was attacked by night."

Tarkhet leaned in, pinning him with cold eyes. "Now be careful what you say. How in eternal night does a retreating army manage an ambush?"

Derkh closed his eyes. He heard again the shouting, saw the confused silhouettes of men running. Felt again Gabrielle's arms about him before she slipped away. "I don't know for sure. I couldn't leave my tent. But maybe it was late-coming reinforcements arriving from another direction. There are four different countries here, you know."

Tarkhet's pale eyes narrowed. He *hadn't* known, Derkh realized. Well, it wasn't exactly a state secret. Be damned if he would tell this bugger anything useful, not if he could help it. His loyalties were clear at last. As far as Derkh was concerned the Almighty Emperor could eat dog turds.

Tarkhet nodded. "I'll accept that for now. Then what happened?"

"They killed my father. Everything seemed confused. I don't really—"

" 'Know anything, because I was injured,' " Tarkhet quoted, snarling. "If you was so badly injured, why ain't you dead? That's the big question, ain't it? Too sick to rise from yer damned bed even during an attack, and here you are large as life and flush with good health!"

"I got better," said Derkh sullenly. That earned him a blow that snapped his head back against the tree trunk and sent the world spinning around him. Blackness bled into the edges of his vision, and he welcomed it.

A pot full of cold water brought him gasping back to daylight.

"The second battle," Tarkhet prodded. "And don't whine to me about your bloody deathbed! Let's say reinforcements *did* arrive, enough to turn the tide. The fact remains that we sent ten thousand troops over the mountains, and only a handful made it back. Are you telling me they slaughtered ten thousand men?"

Not by half, Derkh thought. He pictured the moment in the first battle when he had realized his side was losing men—conscripts melting away through the edges of the enemy ranks like an outgoing tide. Later he had been stunned to learn that, far from being hunted down and put to death, those men were never even pursued. What had happened to them all, he wondered?

Careful, Derkh. He heard the words like a warning bell in his head, and he heard them, oddly enough, in Féolan's voice. Yes, he thought. Let them think the Basin armies are formidable and bloodthirsty. Make them think twice about returning.

"They may be fewer," he whispered. Such an effort it was, to talk against his swelling mouth and the blinding ache in his head. "But they are well equipped and well trained, to a man. They do not send peasants with cast-off swords to fight, but only true soldiers. And it seems," he added, spinning off into fantasy, "that they have no fear, but love battle and take joy in their killing. None were spared."

Too late he realized his mistake.

"Right. None were spared," repeated Tarkhet, each word bitten off and spat out. "So then, my young *injured* son of the man who botched the invasion—how is it that you stand before me? Why is it *you* were spared?"

Tarkhet turned on his heel and strode over to the campfire. "He sold us out to save his skin," he announced flatly. "It's the only explanation.

"Roust, Sturgus." Two men scrambled to their feet and stood to attention. Tarkhet jerked a thumb over his shoulder toward Derkh.

"Kill him."

Dark gods take the brute! Gabrielle's stomach lurched as the heavy fist connected with Derkh's slight body. She heard Féolan's breath expelled in a curse behind her, felt his warning hand on her back. Steady. They were close enough to hear Derkh's anguished groan—like when she first met him, she remembered, so determined not to cry aloud with the pain—but how were two to overpower ten?

They had picked up the trail in the early afternoon, not much more than an hour after taking leave of the *seskeesh*. There were three by then, for the female had left them while Gabrielle slept, and returned with berries, mushrooms and some sort of tuber piled onto a curl of birch bark for her mate. She had been followed by a gangly, nearly full-grown young male who kept a cautious distance between himself and the humans. Their parting had moved Gabrielle beyond words: the way the female had led her to the injured male, awake now and resting comfortably. They had each placed an open palm alongside Gabrielle's face, the dark leathery skin stretching from her chin to the part of her hair. Gazing at her with their strange deep eyes—two as amber as a cat's, two the golden brown of brandy—they had spoken their thanks in guttural sounds she didn't know but seemed to understand all the same. She had laid her own hands, in the same gesture, against their cheeks—downy soft, they were—and then returned to where Féolan waited. But the female had followed them, reached out to stroke Féolan's shoulder, and when he turned in response, touched his face as well. The wonder in his eyes would be one of Gabrielle's favorite memories, she knew.

Those eyes now were dark with anger, the flat gray of storm clouds, as they witnessed Derkh's interrogation.

They had thought the trail they found must have been made by an outpost patrol, who just might have news of Derkh. "They weren't Elves," Féolan had said. "Our scouts don't travel so many together, and in any case would not have torn up the earth so in their passing. I would not have thought it possible to leave such a clear path on this rocky ground."

"Féolan," Gabrielle interrupted. "If our soldiers found him, would they not take him for questioning?"

"Yes, quite possibly," he had replied. "If so, he will at least have shelter and food."

Gabrielle gasped as the next blow connected with Derkh's temple. His head lolled; his face, already purple and swollen with contusions, bled freely from the nose and lip. "Féolan, we have to stop this!"

"We'd have a better chance of escaping with him if he can hold on till dusk," Féolan whispered. "The man is vicious, but he has done no lasting harm yet."

Gabrielle buried her head in her arms where she lay, forcing back the whimpering protest in her throat. She could not bear to watch this until nightfall.

Suddenly Féolan grabbed the bow that lay beside him and leapt to his feet. "Gabrielle, take this knife."

"What—?"

"We just ran out of time. Draw your sword as you go. Use it if you need to. Cut Derkh free and give him the knife. Then get out of here, however you can. If you linger, I swear I'll kill you myself!" He was nocking in an arrow and sighting as he spoke.

SO THAT'S IT then, Derkh thought. Gabrielle might have saved herself the bother for all my life has been worth. The slow stride of the approaching soldiers measured out the distance between himself and his death. He tried to summon up the pride to meet it like a man.

A red star sprouted on Roust's chest, and he staggered and fell. Scurgus turned to look and pitched to his knees, his sword clattering onto the rock, clutching at his throat. His hands flowed red, and Derkh made out the arrow bristling from below his jaw.

A voice spoke to him from behind the tree. It can't be her, he thought wildly. But it was.

"I hope you can walk, Derkh, because I'm cutting these ropes. We have to move fast."

He braced himself against the tree, pressing against it as his legs gave way, and managed to stagger to the far side before they buckled completely. Shouts sounded out now, and Féolan's bow whistled. It must be Féolan, Derkh thought. Gabrielle was rubbing his legs furiously, working out the numbness.

"Take this," she gasped, thrusting the knife handle toward him.

She stooped to sweep up her own sword, then clasped her free arm around his back, supporting his weight.

"Go!" Féolan shouted, and Derkh heard the unmistakable ring of a sword drawn against its sheath. Staggering like a couple of tavern drunks, he and Gabrielle lurched away.

FÉOLAN HAD MANAGED to down just one more pursuer with his bow before their leader called his men back to take cover. Their opponents' new strategy left him with little hope: they had divided into two groups and headed in opposite directions, obviously intending to circle wide and under cover and overtake their quarry from two sides at once.

Sprinting to Derkh's unsupported side, Féolan grabbed the boy's arm and urged him forward. Impossible to outrun men in prime condition, not with Derkh in the state he was. If it was dark they might lose them, but as it was…they would have to fight. But at all costs, they must avoid a two-pronged attack: Derkh and Gabrielle were no match for trained warriors.

Féolan's bright eyes scanned the landscape as they struggled through the rough country. He heard the shouts of the men on each side of them, evenly flanking them now. Once they got a little ahead, they would move in. There had to be a place…

He had it. A narrow approach to a tall cliff face: a rockfall of boulders and rubble piled up on one side, a steep scramble of scree pitching down from the other. They would be trapped there, but at least the enemy would be forced to attack head-on. There was no time for anything better.

DERKH SHOOK FREE of Gabrielle. "It's okay, I'm better now. I can fight." It was fight or die, as his father used to say, and now he discovered the truth of another of Col's sayings: need did, indeed, bring strength. He set his legs and found them surprisingly firm.

"Then you'd better take this," Gabrielle said, handing over her sword. "You're better trained in it than I." She looked over at Féolan. "Should I take your bow?"

"Can you shoot it?"

The Greffaires were approaching openly now, Derkh noticed. Cautious, but confident. Who wouldn't be, he thought dryly, with odds like these? He hefted the sword, getting to know its weight. Lighter than his own had been but beautifully balanced. Wrapping the hilt with the two-handed grip he had been taught, he felt his own confidence take hold. Gabrielle had saved him—again. He would die, and happily, to protect her now.

"I'm better with a bow than a sword. Rosalie gave me some pointers once," Gabrielle replied. Back when archery was about targets, not lives, and I believed I would never deliberately harm another soul, she thought, and clambered onto a low shelf of rock behind them that would give her clear sight-lines.

"Keep it down until I say. Once you are aiming at them, they will have no choice but to charge." Féolan's hand was on his shoulder now. "Ready, Derkh?"

Derkh swallowed. "I'm ready. Féolan, Gabrielle—I have put you in danger. I am sorry."

"We came of our own free will, Derkh—no blame to you. Now we must save each other."

No time for more. The men were pounding toward them. The bow sang in Derkh's ears, and one man checked mid-stride, clutching his shoulder. Then the rest were upon them, and Derkh was fighting for his life against his own people—for his life, and the lives of his friends.

CHAPTER SIXTEEN

ONE, even two or three, would have posed little problem. Powerful men though they were, the Greffaires could not match Féolan's Elvish speed and agility in hand-to-hand combat. But seven...they were simply too many. Féolan could fend off several at a time, but it was devilish hard to strike a blow against one while defending against others. Gabrielle's one bowshot must have struck the studded leather strapping across the man's chest, for he had fallen back only briefly. Féolan had managed to put one attacker out of action with a slash through the middle and had ruined another's sword-hand. It was not enough, and he knew it.

He stole another glance at Derkh and Gabrielle. They were holding their own, but he could feel Derkh's fatigue. After what the boy had been through, his strength could not last long. Once the Greffaires had closed in, Gabrielle had given up the bow and was now doing what she could to aid Derkh with Féolan's long-bladed knife.

They would die here, all three of them. Regret, as bitter as bile, filled him: to have brought Gabrielle on this fruitless journey. He parried, parried, the endless rain of blows. A clash of steel rang out beside him; he flashed a look to see Gabrielle's knife blade raised high, braced against a sword-stroke destined for Derkh's skull, saw Derkh take the opening and thrust. Good, lad! Féolan kicked at another Greffaire moving in on Derkh. It accomplished only a momentary stagger, but it bought the time the boy needed. Gods, he deserved a better end than this. They all did.

The knife as it flew was no more than a flicker in his peripheral vision. Only Gabrielle's cry told him what he had seen.

NONE OF THEM noticed when Tarkhet fell back from the fray and pulled his knife. To Gabrielle it seemed rather that the blade burst from beneath her skin, some disastrous, inexplicable rupture of her own body. She had fallen back against the cliff face before she knew what was wrong with her. It was her hands, instinctively clutching at the hurt place, that discovered a knife hilt jutting from under her sternum. Tarkhet had thrown it at the exposed sweep of her body while she stretched up to block that last blow.

"I'm all right!" she yelled. Tried to yell. She wasn't all right, she knew that already, but they mustn't know it. All would be lost if they came to her now.

Appalling, how her fingers fluttered so uselessly at the blade, how deep and agonizing its bite. How the blood welled into her hands until they lay hidden in a slick pool.

Healer, see to thy own wounds. Her old teacher Marcus's words were commanding, but Gabrielle's mind was too frightened and confused to obey. The noise of the fighting boomed and receded in her head. Pain clawed away her thoughts. Focus eluded her.

Gabrielle took a slow, painful breath and another, trying to clear the mist that was creeping into the corners of her vision. She groped for the healing light that had served her so often on behalf of others. She could not tell if she slipped into trance or oblivion, but she was beyond stopping it. Her eyes closed, and the roars and screams of battle faded away.

SO IT WAS that Gabrielle never witnessed the event that Derkh and Féolan could only speak of afterward in halting awestruck words.

Derkh and Féolan stood shoulder-to-shoulder against four men, black-hearted, thinking now only to exact a high price for their lives.

And then it was as if some raging storm flew in among them, a deafening wind that scattered men before it like so many leaves. Their assailants flew like rag dolls into the air, crashing down against boulder and scree. Only one was able to rise again to make his terrified escape.

Féolan's firm hand restraining his sword-arm was all that stood between Derkh and panic. He did not know, afterward, if he would have tried to flee or attack. As it was, he stood paralyzed, beyond speech or rational thought.

"They are *seskeesh*, rare creatures of the high mountains," muttered Féolan. "I do not know why they have come down so far, but they are friends." The amber eyes that appraised him now did not strike Derkh as especially friendly, and alarm clamored in him as the larger of the huge beasts shouldered past and hunkered down beside Gabrielle. Féolan made no move to stop it (as if anyone could!) but followed to Gabrielle's side. I forgot about her, Derkh thought, sick now with grief at the sight of her still form.

He watched Féolan feel the pulse in Gabrielle's neck, smooth back her hair, kiss her white brow. Only when the giant creature laid a hairy finger on Féolan's cheek did Derkh see that he was weeping. Féolan reached up, laid his hand on the shaggy wrist and spoke quietly in Elvish.

Making the strangest noise, a noise Derkh could only call

crooning though deeper than any man's voice, the *seskeesh* scooped up Gabrielle's limp body as easily as Derkh would a baby and strode off.

"Let's go," said Féolan. "We'll get her to shelter first, and then see if there's anything I can do for her." His voice was so tight that Derkh didn't dare ask more. He did his best to master his shaking legs and followed.

THE *SESKEESH* DID not lead them back to the cleft in the rock where they had first met her, as Féolan expected. Instead, she and her companion led them almost due north into higher country. Fifteen minutes of hard climbing—fifteen minutes that seemed an age to Féolan, anxious as he was to tend to Gabrielle—and they stood before the gaping mouth of a high-ceilinged cave. The two *seskeesh* strode in, while Féolan and Derkh hesitated just inside the entrance, blinded momentarily by the sudden dimness. The air inside was thick with the musky animal odor of the *seskeesh*, and something fresher: the resinous smell of evergreens.

Féolan picked his way after the *seskeesh*. She was about to lay Gabrielle on a pile of balsam branches stacked against the stone wall of the cave. "Wait," he said. Amber eyes, eerily lambent in the gloom, regarded him. Pulling the cloak from his pack, he spread it out over the branches. "Now."

His mind raced as he bent over her still form. She breathed still. Her pulse was quick and thready. The knife hung beneath her rib cage. He could not sense the bright mind he loved. Scrabbly disconnected thoughts flickered in Féolan's mind, and he forced himself to put them aside. *I cannot help her if I fall apart.*

Reaching for Gabrielle's pack, he emptied it beside him, identifying each item more by feel than sight. Yes, here a cloth bag full of clean bandaging. Here a smaller bag with packets of herbs. Did she go anywhere without them?

"I need hot water for a poultice." He spoke to himself, and the hand on his shoulder—a fleeting, shy touch—startled him momentarily. He had all but forgotten Derkh.

"I'll take care of it," said the boy, and Féolan looked up gratefully, only to be shocked anew at the extent of Derkh's hurts. His face was unrecognizable, an angry welt of injury, and even in the dim light of the cave exhaustion was plain to read in his eyes and posture.

"Derkh. You should be getting care yourself. I'm sorry—"

An impatient headshake cut him off. "I'm sore, that's all. Not dying. I'll get wood." And he was gone.

Precious minutes ticked by while Féolan struggled to make the *seskeesh* comprehend the need for fire. *For medicine. For her life.* He thought, in the end, she had given permission as long as the fire was outside the cave. He hoped so.

While wood was gathered and laid, and water set to heat, Féolan merely sat with Gabrielle, trying to send strength to her, trying not to be frightened by the eerie sense that she was absent from her own body.

"It's boiling now, Féolan." Derkh's voice was hushed, his own fear now plain. Gathering up the medicine bags, Féolan followed him outside.

"Let's see…" Flipping through the labeled packets, he pulled out those he recognized. "Comfrey, goldenseal, good. Rattleroot—I don't know what that is. Willowbark is more for a fever drink, I think. Hawkweed…"

Was it the hawkweed he had gathered with Gabrielle a year ago? He could see the field now, a grassy sky dotted with blazing orange stars. He couldn't remember what she said it was for, but he would use it anyway. For luck. For love.

Careful to keep the bandage cloths from trailing on the ground, he sorted through until he found one big enough to fold into an envelope around the assortment of herbs. He tied it securely, and handed it to Derkh.

"Put it gently in the boiling water, then take the pot off the heat. When it's cool enough that you can put your hand against the pot without burning, bring the whole thing in to me."

There could be no more delays. It was time.

GABRIELLE WANDERED IN a dark, featureless land. She walked directionless, blind, not knowing what else to do. Her home was lost to her. Longing squeezed her heart, but already what she longed for grew vague and shapeless. She was between worlds, she knew: on the journey of the dead.

Gabrielle.

She lifted her head. Had she imagined it?

Gabrielle, hear me. Come back.

Féolan? Féolan, I'm lost.

You are found. Gabrielle, follow me. Come back.

Her feet had stopped their dreary trudging. She turned, almost reluctantly. It was so far. And…she remembered now. It hurt back there, hurt worse than anything in her memory.

Féolan, I'm afraid.

The reply was urgent, almost angry. It set her direction like a beacon light on a foggy coast.

You are a healer, and you are needed! Do not abandon your body before its time. Come back to me!

His mind now was like a thread of light pulling her back.

Gabrielle grasped the gleaming thread, and followed.

THE PAIN WAS a fire in her breast, red and raging. It blocked out every other thought.

You are not the pain. You are yourself.

She struggled to rise above the flames that burned within her. New strength seeped into her as Féolan lent his own energy to her effort.

Light careful breaths from the abdomen eased the searing bite of each rush of indrawn air. Gabrielle gathered her concentration. *You are not the pain.* She felt her mind come back as the familiar ritual engaged her. *Diagnose the injury.*

She focused in. The blade appeared in her mind's vision as a black emptiness thrust deep into living tissue. The shock of it—her own body rent so—threatened to overwhelm her. Talons of fear gripped at her. *I can't. I'm too hurt. Too weak.* The dark place called: a place, it seemed now, of comfort. Of release.

Attend to the patient! Marcus's gruff voice was a terse command. *Attend to the patient, as you have vowed to do.* The old words of the Bonemender's Oath, words she herself had recited and meant with all her heart, sounded like a trumpet call: *To attend to the patient above all concerns, unswayed by the winds of politics or prospect of recompense...* The complete oath took shape in her mind, formed in the same elegant script that engraved the pewter vessel Marcus had given her to mark the end of her training. Gabrielle had never abandoned a patient yet. She would not do so now.

Layer by layer, she explored the damage. It was injury to the diaphragm, not her lung as she had feared, that made her breath burn. That would heal. The blade had plunged through the upper section of the liver, angling toward her left side to nick the top shoulder of the stomach, and then—*oh, Marcus, help me.*

Her life hung by a thread, or rather a knife tip. If it had not been a short blade, the kind designed to lie hidden along a man's forearm, she would be dead even now. As it was, the tip lay embedded in the lower heart path artery, the great artery running from the heart through the trunk of the body. Though much blood had escaped, especially when the knife had been jarred during the trip to the cave, the blade still made an imperfect plug, holding back the powerful gushes that would otherwise have burst from the wound. A quarter-inch of steel was all that stood between Gabrielle and a quick and bloody death.

FÉOLAN TOOK A deep breath. He had cut away the bloody cloth around the wound and sponged it off as best he could. Derkh kneeled beside him with a pressure pad of bandaging.

Gabrielle. He could feel her presence now, though she felt far away. Far away, working, he hoped. *Gabrielle, I'm going to pull out the blade now.*

The alarmed reaction was almost like a blow. She leapt into his mind, her urgency unmistakable. *NO!* Féolan frowned, confused. Was it just her fear? It didn't feel like fear. And she knew as well as he a knife could not be left in a wound.

She was speaking now, trying to. He bent low, his ear brushing her lips.

The word was barely a breath, but it was clear enough. "Wait."

CHAPTER SEVENTEEN

"WHAT does Uncle Tristan say?" Matthieu's eyes were trained on his father, Dominic. Dominic's eyes were trained on the parchment just delivered into his hands, and his lips were set in the straight thin line that signaled anger.

"He says, let's see…that everyone is fine, and that he is bringing Rosalie and her father back here for a visit."

"That's not all!" protested Matthieu. "Look how much he wrote!"

"That's all for boys," replied Dominic firmly. He glanced at Solange, tucked into her favorite rocking chair by the fire with baby Sylvain, and shook his head.

"Matthieu, I told you," Madeleine piped up, exasperated, "you shouldn't ask. It's better to be really, really quiet, so they forget you're there. That's the only way to find out stuff grown-ups don't want you to know!"

"A strategy that I have used myself to good effect, many times," said Solange, smiling. "This time, however, we remembered you." She reached out her hand for the parchment and read the letter herself—silently.

THE NEWS COULD not be kept from the children for long. Normand, for one, was so outraged by the assassination attempt that he could not have kept quiet about it to save his life.

Soon most of Chênier would be buzzing with the news, and so Madeleine and Matthieu were told the contents of Tristan's letter after all, albeit a glossed-over version.

"He's a bad man, isn't he, Mama?" said Matthieu as Justine came to the end of her account, and Solange, overhearing, surprised them with an uncharacteristic outburst.

"There isn't a word in any language bad enough for that man!" she declared and swept out of the room.

Tristan had been right to suggest leaving Blanchette. Away from the scene of the attack, it was easier to shake off the shadow of what had happened. And even with LaBarque safely imprisoned, Rosalie and André were grateful for the security of the castle. "It's just nice to go to bed at night and not have to wonder if it's okay to fall asleep," explained Rosalie. Justine nodded sympathetically, snugging her sleeping baby tight against her body as if he might be the next victim.

They were in the kitchen, working out the menu for the next day's picnic excursion into the hills. The outing had been Solange's suggestion—another surprise—and everyone had welcomed it immediately. "We all need cheering up," she said. "And high summer is upon us. We should get out into the air and sunshine. It would not please your father to see me shut myself behind stone walls and refuse the gifts of nature."

THE DAY WAS fair and golden, and thanks to their grouchy but devoted cook they ate very well indeed. So well, in fact, that afterward most of the adults were inclined to drowse in the sun and recover.

Matthieu and Madeleine surveyed the lolling grown-ups with disgust. André sat against a tree, his face covered with a napkin.

Their mother lay on a blanket in the shade, baby Sylvain at her breast. Dominic sat beside them, awake but distinctly dopey-looking. Solange, Tristan and Rosalie talked quietly together. Matthieu summed up the verdict with one word:

"Boring."

He looked at Madeleine, grinned, and launched himself at Tristan.

"OOOF!"

Rosalie let out a startled shriek as Tristan collapsed beside her, propelled by fifty pounds of boy. She watched the ensuing wrestling match with amusement—Tristan was having a hard time holding his own against such overwhelming enthusiasm. At last Matthieu, heaving and giggling, was duly pinned and released, "On your own recognizance, mind."

"Uncle Tristan," begged the boy.

"What now, you bundle of trouble?"

"Tell us again how you beat that guy—LaBarque."

"And Rosalie too," prompted Madeleine. "She beat him too."

"She did, indeed!" agreed Tristan. He had never been able to resist a good story, thought Rosalie, as he launched into a re-enactment of the scene.

"So then I *dove* under the table and grabbed his chair!" Tristan, already on his knees, ploughed into the delighted Matthieu and flipped him over. "And then we wrestled"—great scuffling and grunts—"until finally I hauled him to his feet with his own knife against his throat"—and there he stood, one arm wrapped around the giggling boy's chest and his index finger tucked under his chin.

Rosalie caught Madeleine's eye and rolled her eyes. "Boys," she said, and Madeleine nodded knowingly, though her grin was as wide as Matthieu's, and her eyes shone with excitement. Then Rosie happened to glance at Solange, and her own smile faded. Solange stared at the horizon as if she didn't hear, but her distress was plain to see. Her whole body was rigid with tension, her lips pressed together hard.

"Tristan." Rosalie reached out and tapped Tristan's calf. He glanced at her, distracted. "Not now," she said softly.

"Aw, Rosie." He threw her the devil-may-care grin that she had always found charming—until today. "Don't be so stuffy. We're just playing around, aren't we, Matthieu?" And turning his back on her, he launched into Scene Two of Tristan Saves the Day.

Anger ran so hot at his off-hand dismissal that her cheeks burned with it. *You childish, self-absorbed, unthinking, rude...* Her mind ran out of words to shout, and all she had done was glare and turn red in the face.

Abruptly she remembered Solange. She turned—but Solange was on her feet. Dashing a cheek with the back of her hand, walking with the dignity she never seemed to lose, she headed over to the "lookout chair" that had been carved into a natural stone formation that offered a view of Chênier and the Avine River.

Rosalie watched her go, helpless, wondering what she should do. She looked around for Justine, but Justine was soothing Sylvain to sleep. Rosalie didn't know Tristan's mother well enough to know if she should follow or respect her solitude.

She glared again at Tristan, still goofing with the kids, still oblivious. He should be the one going over there. Oaf, she thought. Firing off one last, withering but completely ignored look, she screwed up her courage and followed Solange.

"I DO NOT think I will ever be able to joke about that," said Solange as Rosalie approached. Rosalie sat quietly beside the older woman.

"I'm sorry you had to hear it," she said. "Tristan should have thought—"

"Tristan has his own way of dealing with troubles. But I cannot bear to think of what might have been. For my husband to give his life in battle, and my children to risk theirs, only to be repaid in such kind!"

They sat in silence for a while, looking over the sweep of land, feeling the sun's warmth and the sweet breezes. Then Solange turned and looked at Rosalie for the first time. "If that man had had his way and taken my son in his treachery, I do not know how I could have continued. There is not enough courage left in me to face such a loss."

Rosalie's own eyes stung with tears. Her own awkwardness forgotten, she leaned over and brushed the older woman's cheek with a quick kiss before returning to the picnic.

Tristan was lying on a sun-drenched rock, chewing on an apple. The kids, apparently, had gone off on an adventure of their own. He hoisted himself onto one elbow as Rosalie came near and squinted across the meadow at Solange.

"What was that all about?" he asked.

"Open your eyes, Tristan!" Rosalie snapped. "Everything is not a game!" Tossing her dark ringlets, she stalked off to join Justine. Tristan stared after her, his face a caricature of baffled innocence.

"And what was *that* all about?"

CHAPTER EIGHTEEN

THEY lived among the *seskeesh* for nearly a fortnight. For the first week Gabrielle hardly roused, alternating between sleep and the apparent-sleep of her healing trance. Féolan and Derkh did little but keep vigil for the first two days, subsisting on Féolan's remaining supplies.

On the third day, when Gabrielle seemed less likely to die at any moment, Féolan left the cave for some time. He returned with a straight shoulder-high branch, which he proceeded to lash to one of his arrows. When he was satisfied with his work, he tossed the makeshift spear to Derkh.

"Ever gone fishing?" he asked.

"Sure," Derkh replied dubiously. "But not with one of these."

"Then this is your big chance to learn," announced Féolan. "The stream where the *seskeesh* drink is full of trout. It's time we dug for our dinner."

"Are we out of food?" asked Derkh.

"Not really. There is plenty of travel biscuit still—we packed extra, so as to outfit you better if you really were bent on leaving us. But it makes for a dreary diet, day after day."

Derkh turned away abruptly, hiding his face. He was still Greffaire enough to be mortified at the way his throat tightened with this news. He had not really considered why Féolan and Gabrielle had followed him so far into the mountains, but as he trudged to the nearby brook he realized that he had assumed it was to prevent his departure. But it wasn't. They had come to help him.

His mind was a kaleidoscope of memories: Gabrielle, exhausted and grief-stricken, laboring to the point of collapse to save Derkh's life. Féolan, peering into the cart where Derkh lay feverish, taking him not to the executioner but to the surgeon's tents. Féolan kneeling before him, offering his own life for the slaying of Derkh's father. Gabrielle's quiet hurt, when he refused her table. How often must they prove their friendship, before you will trust in it?

The trout proved as elusive as quicksilver, flashing away from his spear almost before it broke the water. But Derkh was determined that, in this at least, he would not fail his friend, and by late afternoon he had caught two smallish fish and a large bullfrog. He returned to the cave just as Féolan was changing the bandages on Gabrielle's still form.

"That's a good start," Féolan said with a nod.

The little catch caused quite a stir among the three *seskeesh*. The female poked at Derkh's catch, and then left the cave with the young male. They were back before the sun was down with a heap of bloody fish—a dozen at least.

Féolan's grin, broad and untroubled, was worth being shown up for. "Looks like you've met your match, my boy. Though I wager you cook better than they do."

The tables were turned later that week, when Féolan emerged from the woods with a deer slung over his shoulders. The *seskeesh* were clearly amazed, and when Féolan separated a back haunch for himself and Derkh, then turned the rest of the carcass over to his hosts, they crowded around noisily, patting him so enthusiastically on the head and back in their excitement that Derkh feared a little for his safety.

When at last the *seskeesh* retreated with their prize, Féolan and Derkh turned back to Gabrielle. She was awake, watching them—and she was smiling. When she spoke, her voice was weak but clear. "I see you have become one of the family," she said.

GABRIELLE WORKED UNTIL she must rest, and rested until she could work. For days her life held to this elemental rhythm, interrupted only for the briefest waking to sip some water or broth, or to empty her bladder. The work was exhausting, weakened as she was, and the balance delicate: She must not push herself too hard or risk collapse, yet she dared not leave such a wound unattended for long. The first long night, she thought only to mend and strengthen the heart-path puncture. It had taken a huge effort just to prepare for the drawing of the weapon. She had made a weak join in the tear where it had widened each side of the blade and then envisioned a kind of mental brace of healing light behind the artery wall, ready to be lashed together as the knife tip retreated. That was her moment of greatest danger. Though she threw the full force of her mind against it, the wall she had created barely held, so powerful was the surge of blood. It had taken the last of her will and strength to make a patch too flimsy to stand up to the least movement. She would not normally have trusted a patient for two minutes to such a weak vessel wall, but she had no choice. As oblivion swallowed her she had just one prayer—that she would sleep quietly.

Day by day, Gabrielle's stamina improved and the periods of healing grew longer. As her exhaustion eased, however, the pain pressed in harder on her consciousness. Her sleep was uneasy now, every inadvertent movement stabbing her awake. And waking was a trial she wanted to endure as infrequently as possible.

Day and night held little meaning in this twilight existence, so she did not know that nearly a week had passed when the uproar from the *seskeesh* prodded her awake. She only knew she felt better: the pain was a steady companion, not a consuming fire. And she was hungry. At the thought of food her stomach cramped and yawned, and Gabrielle realized that her shaky weakness was at least partly due to her long fast.

Féolan and Derkh both seemed overcome to see Gabrielle awake and lucid. They must have kept a long vigil, she thought, as she watched Derkh's bruised eyes fill with tears. Féolan was bent over her hand and seemed unable to speak. Her heart twisted, and she felt her own throat prickle and tighten.

"Don't," Gabrielle gasped. "Don't make me cry. It will hurt like blazes. Please!"

Derkh dashed his eyes with the back of a hand and managed a wan smile.

"Your face still looks awful," offered Gabrielle.

The smile broadened. "There wasn't any healer around to take care of me," he explained.

Gabrielle was tiring already. She closed her eyes and managed one last piece of conversation:

"If that was meat I saw in that fracas, I hope you saved some for me. Turn it into something a sick person can eat, and I will sing your praises forever."

GABRIELLE WAS STILL in no shape to hike, when they left the cave six days later, but she didn't have to. She was carried tenderly to within a few miles of the Skyway Pass and as far south into the Maronnais hills as the shy *seskeesh* dared venture. The great female laid her into Féolan's waiting arms, caressed her face with a giant hand and slipped away. Gabrielle knew there was no need for further words or gestures—nestled in the great creature's arms, she had sent her thanks every step of the long way—but she still could not stay her weeping.

"Where to now?" asked Derkh.

"A track skirts the mountains the length of La Maronne," answered Féolan. "It's not much more than a footpath, but locals and supply carts do travel it. We'll rest there and hope to flag down a cart for Gabrielle."

"From there to the outpost by the Skyway Pass, I suppose?" Derkh's face darkened at the prospect of facing more suspicious soldiers.

"Don't worry, Derkh. It will be all right." Gabrielle sniffed up her tears and smiled at Derkh. He brightened in response. He had changed, Gabrielle realized, remembering his tears in the cave. Some of the prickly self-protective caution had been left behind in the mountains.

Féolan winked at Derkh, adjusted Gabrielle's weight and started trudging south. "She's right, lad. If you're going to make friends in Verdeau, the king's daughter is a pretty good place to start."

CHAPTER NINETEEN

"**B**UT I didn't know she was upset!" protested Tristan, exasperated.

A dinner, an evening and a breakfast spent in Rosalie's polite but frosty company had been all Tristan could stand. He had finally pulled her into an empty room, closed the door and demanded, "Why are you mad at me?" Now he had his answer, but he still couldn't fathom it.

"You *should* have known," retorted Rosalie.

"But I didn't. I can't make myself know something that I don't know! I was playing with the kids; I didn't notice her."

"Right."

"Huh?"

"You didn't even notice her. And then you didn't notice me. All you noticed was your own little game. When are you going to grow up and think about the people around you? Your mother has been through a lot lately, in case you hadn't *noticed*."

Tristan flared into anger. "What do you know about my mother? Or me? Gods on fire, you have a nerve!" Catching himself yelling, he broke off and forced himself to speak quietly. It didn't come out reasonable and calm, though. It came out tight and accusing.

"I know more about the pain my mother carries than you ever will. I was there when she learned of my father's death. I never claimed to be perfect—but don't you tell me I don't care about my own family!"

He was out the door and halfway up the staircase before Rosalie could say another word.

TRISTAN FROWNED AT the parchment spread out before him.

"The talks are in Gaudette? Why so far?"

"The Barilles general and his party want to be close to the pass, so they can examine the battle sites," Dominic explained.

"Why do they want to do that?"

Dominic shrugged. "They say it's to understand the tactical situation. Personally, I think they can't quite believe the attack really happened." He looked up and caught Tristan's incredulous look. "Not that they think we are lying about it. Why would we? But you can understand how the threat might not seem real to them, Tris. And maybe they doubt the scope of what we are reporting."

"Hmm. Well, whatever. We need them to be part of this, so if they want to troop up to Gaudette, so be it."

"That's about the size of it," agreed Dominic. "So the next question is, are you going? You were keen to represent us at these talks before our merchant friend threw a wrench in things. Do you want to take over from here?"

"Yeah, I do," said Tristan slowly. "Only… It's twice as far as Ratigouche. We'll have to head out quite soon. When does General Fortin plan to leave?"

"Three days from now. He wants to arrive a little early and make sure everything is prepared." Dominic noted Tristan's glum look. "What?"

"It's Rosie," admitted Tristan. "We haven't exactly been getting along well lately. I just hate to leave with bad feelings between us."

"Had a lover's quarrel, have you?"

Tristan declined to answer. His sibling's tendency to make light of his love life was starting to annoy him.

"Well, you have three days to patch things up. That should be plenty," remarked Dominic.

"Plenty if you know how," Tristan answered morosely. He dropped his head onto one hand, a fistful of blond hair sprouting between his fingers, and peered up at Dominic. "You've been married a long time. Don't you and Justine ever fight?"

"Of course we do."

"So how do you stop?"

Dominic regarded his brother's tufted hair. "I presume you've apologized."

"Apologized?" Tristan sat up abruptly. "Why should I? I didn't even *do* anything!"

"You haven't apologized." Dominic shook his head. "You don't know much about this, do you?"

"But I didn't do anything wrong! I mean, I guess I did, but I couldn't help it."

"Irrelevant."

"What do you mean, irrelevant?"

"Do you want to make up with her?"

"Yes, but—"

"Then the rest is irrelevant. Apologize. Even if you don't know what you did, apologize for it."

"But—"

"It's code, Tristan," Dominic said firmly. "Think of it as code."

"Code for what?"

"Code for, 'I'm sorry we made each other feel bad, and I want us to be happy again.'"

Tristan pondered this brotherly wisdom for a minute.

"Does Rosie know it's code? Or will she take it as an admission of fault?"

"It doesn't matter," insisted Dominic. "Look, if the code doesn't do it for you, just picture heading off into the reaches of La Maronne without so much as a goodbye kiss."

Tristan gave his hair a hasty rake down with both hands, rolled up the manuscript and stood.

"Point made, big brother. All right, I'm off to apologize. In code."

"One last pointer? By way of hard-earned personal experience?"

"Why not? Shoot."

"Don't say, 'I'm sorry but.' Just say you're sorry. Period."

Tristan sighed. "I'm gonna feel like a cat choking on a hair ball." He padded off in search of Rosalie.

Dominic's encouraging smile spread into a grin as Tristan disappeared down the hall. Wouldn't I love to be a fly on the wall for this little chat! he thought. Probably the first apology Tristan has ever made.

THE HAIR BALL proved less hard to spit out than Tristan had feared, and its gracious reception did much to soothe his wounded pride.

"I'm sorry too, Tris," said Rosalie into his chest. He didn't even remember her getting up from the lawn swing she had been perched on, but she must have because here she was in his arms. Maybe they were pulled together like magnets. "I said things I shouldn't have, that I had no right to."

"Hey, that's okay." Tristan pulled her tighter and nuzzled into her hair, marveling at his brother's perception. He had never thought of Dominic as especially brilliant, if the truth be known. More in the reliable-but-dull category. He would have to rethink that opinion now.

TRISTAN WAS CLOSETED with General Fortin, reviewing the list of delegates for the upcoming defense talks and the proposals they would put forward.

"I think it's good, after all, that we are meeting in La Maronne," he offered. "As the entry point for the Greffaires, the Maronnais have the most at stake. It makes sense that they should host it."

Fortin nodded agreement. "There is one last question I wished to discuss with you, Sire. Our first meeting—the one Prince Dominic attended—proved somewhat chaotic."

"Yes, that was Dominic's assessment too."

"It is new to us, this business of planning among four different nations," continued Fortin, "four heads of state and four generals, all of them used to taking the lead and dominating in a discussion."

"All of them with their contingent of aides and courtiers, each one bent on making his mark," added Tristan dryly.

"Precisely."

"Is there a solution?"

"I was going to suggest we propose appointing a director of the talks. The director's role is not to put forward his own opinion, but to keep the discussion orderly. People would require the acknowledgment of the director to speak, and he would also be responsible for summarizing any conclusions and confirming the agreement of all parties."

"Big job," said Tristan. "You know what the difficulty is?"

"Sire?"

"It would have to be a prominent, respected person. If things get heated, he may have to refuse or even reprimand the highest-ranking personages in the Krylian Basin. Right?"

"Yes, that's true," agreed Fortin.

"But none of the important people there will wish to play that role because it will limit their ability to promote their own viewpoint."

They were interrupted by a knock on the door. Dominic stuck his head in.

"Can I interrupt?"

"Of course," said Tristan. "What's up?"

Dominic entered the room and waved a roll of parchment at them.

"This just arrived from Blanchette. You won't believe it."

CHAPTER TWENTY

CART traffic was sparse along the little track that meandered along the northern edge of La Maronne, but just as Féolan had concluded that he would have to carry Gabrielle all the way to the Skyway Outpost, a herd of sheep made their way down the path, followed by a weather-beaten shepherd pulling a hand cart piled with clothing, blankets and supplies.

There was no need to impress the man with Gabrielle's lineage. He took one look at Gabrielle ("so fair, wan and wounded," Féolan would joke, later), scratched at his ample beard as if deep in thought and began unpacking his wagon. Most items were tied into a blanket and slung over his back. Féolan and Derkh tucked what they could into their packs. With a grand gesture, their new friend motioned Gabrielle to the empty, and rather rickety-looking, hand cart.

"Will it do, Gabrielle?" asked Féolan, worried. "I think it's only a few more miles, but that thing will be bumpy beyond belief, and there isn't room to lie down."

"They're all bumpy beyond belief," said Gabrielle. "Big or small. I wonder, though, if we might be able to rig up a little backrest. It would help if I had something to lean against."

A pack filled with cloaks and blankets was tucked behind her, and she was soon being hauled down the road, legs dangling behind, surrounded by milling sheep.

It was the slowest part of the journey for Féolan. He could see Gabrielle tire from the effort of bracing herself against the pitch of the little cart, see her face tighten in pain with every rattle. He would rather have carried her, but after three hours of rocky downhill track he couldn't manage much more.

Abruptly the wagon stopped, and with a yell the shepherd bolted off the track after a group of straying sheep. Féolan crouched in front of Gabrielle's knees and looked up into her face. "How are you doing?" he asked.

"Let's just say it's not *seskeesh* travel," said Gabrielle. "I'll be bloody glad to get off this thing. But I'll last."

Their friend was stumping back, brandishing his hat behind four reluctant sheep. Waving off Derkh's offer to take a turn, he hoisted up the handles of the cart and offered them a wide, gap-toothed smile. "Stupid beasts," he said. And then, "Goin' to the soldiers' camp?" They were the first—and only—words he spoke to them.

Squinting into the late-afternoon sun, they rattled down the road.

THE SENTRY WHO intercepted them swept his eyes over the trio, noting the green and yellow mottles of Derkh's fading bruises and Gabrielle's exhausted slump, and raised a hand to forestall Féolan's explanations.

"You'd be the Elf-fellow, Féolan, and this the king's daughter of Verdeau," he surmised, in the clipped tones of Marronaise Krylaise. "And you," he continued, pointing a thick finger at Derkh, "would be the lad they were looking for." He nodded with satisfaction at the three stunned faces. "Only thing I don't get is, who's this one?" he asked, gesturing at the shepherd.

"Mutton delivery, ten head, to the Chief Provisioner," the man replied, and then looked indignant at the ensuing laughter.

"That's the biggest herd of ten I ever saw," remarked the sentry.

Féolan stepped in. "This man very kindly provided transport to the Lady Gabrielle, and we owe him a great debt of gratitude." The shepherd, who had previously waved away their offer of payment as imperiously as he had waved Derkh away from the cart, puffed with pleasure.

"How did you know about us?" Féolan asked, as the sentry escorted them to the camp.

"A friend of yours was here, looking for you," the man replied. "Says you was late returning and asked us to watch. He's up the mountain right now, searching, but he'll be back, I warrant."

Living conditions in the outpost were rough, but a vast improvement to sleeping on rock and cooking over a fire. Though the outpost men were still housed in tents, a row of wooden cabins was being built to provide year-round shelter. In just minutes, mattresses were moved into the most finished of these, a set of real sheets proudly produced by the on-site Commander, and Gabrielle was soon comfortably tucked in. She was asleep almost instantly and did not rouse until morning.

"WAKE UP, SLEEPYHEAD. You've missed dinner and are very close to missing breakfast. That's no way to build up your strength." Gabrielle's eyes fluttered open. She knew this voice, knew she would turn her head to find warm brown eyes, golden hair, a fair Elvish face.

"Danaïs. You seem determined always to see me at my worst." In the short time of their friendship, Danaïs had seen Gabrielle heartbroken, exhausted and filthy beyond belief.

He laughed, the sound a merry soft cascade. "You were much worse than this just days ago, or so I am told."

"True, I'm afraid." She stretched experimentally. "I am hungry, though. Do you think…?"

"I do not think. I am certain. Féolan and Derkh are vying even now to see who can haul back the largest, most sumptuous breakfast for you. You will have to settle for filling rather than sumptuous, though. It's soldier fare here, plain and simple."

Féolan and Derkh shouldered in, bearing great trays of food, and as they ate Danaïs took the opportunity to fill them in on his part of the story. "When you did not return in almost two weeks, I decided to look for you. And it seemed smarter by then to start at the end of your journey, so I rode straight here."

"You could search these mountains for three months and never find anyone," remarked Féolan.

"Yes, but I did not have three months, so it is well you found yourselves," retorted Danaïs. "The First Ambassador may have forgotten, but his Council has not, that the next joint defense talks with the Humans take place in less than a week." Féolan's expression was comically transparent. "You *had* forgotten, I see. Perhaps you have forgotten also that it is to be held quite close to here, in Gaudette. So I was charged, in the unfortunate event that you were not found, to take your place as Ambassador and Translator for the Elvish Defense Council." He chewed for a bit, considering.

"It's rather a pity you showed up, now I think about it. I was looking forward to rubbing shoulders with the Great."

Under the laughter, Danaïs's gentle gaze took in the way Féolan's eyes kept returning to Gabrielle, checking, he knew, for signs of fever, fatigue, pain.

"Derkh," he said. "Let's you and me clear away this mighty mess and leave these two in peace a while. We can go to my tent or find a rock in the sun, and you can satisfy my curiosity there."

TELLING DANAÏS WHAT had happened to them all, from beginning to end, was probably the longest Derkh had ever talked in his life.

He had been worried that Danaïs would, in his light-hearted way, make a joke of his tale. But his fears were unfounded. To his relief, the Elf allowed Derkh to tell the story in his own way, waiting patiently when he groped to find a Krylaise word or lapsed into Greffaire, interrupting only to clarify when he didn't understand. It was another thing Derkh was learning from his new friends: that qualities he had been raised to see as contradictory could co-exist. A person could be both serious and silly, or like the *seskeesh*, powerful and gentle. First he told the facts, unembellished with his own opinions or feelings, the way he had been taught to report on military action. And then, encouraged somehow by Danaïs's silent attentiveness, he surprised himself by telling more.

"Maybe the real reason I left was because I couldn't believe that anyone here could really be my friend. It didn't seem to matter what they did; I couldn't believe in it. And then Gabrielle nearly died trying to save me, and Féolan never said one word of blame. I don't know what I would have done if she had died. But she lived, and I know now that all the shame and regret I have for what happened will not give her any satisfaction, only more pain. I think, if I want to repay this debt, the only way is to try to give back to her what she has given me all along. To be her friend." Derkh swallowed, struggling against his own embarrassment, and finally lifted his dark eyes to meet Danaïs's.

The Elf contemplated him in silence, and Derkh kept his head up and allowed the scrutiny. At last Danaïs smiled and shook his head gently, and Derkh's own grin of relief was wide enough to hurt his bruised cheeks. He felt light, like he'd laid down a heavy pack that had bent him to the ground.

"I foretold, if you remember, a growth spurt for you," said Danaïs. Derkh didn't follow at first. "At Gabrielle's dinner," prompted Danaïs. "When you were piling your plate to the sky."

"Oh, I remember now," said Derkh. The night he almost changed his mind, that was. The night he almost believed.

"I was right, was I not? You have grown tall indeed. Tall in here." He reached over and laid a hand over Derkh's heart. It was a touch Derkh might have flinched away from not long ago. Now he accepted it, seeing in his mind's eye the way the *seskeesh* had cradled Gabrielle's face in its great hand, the dignity and tenderness of the gesture.

"I would be proud, Derkh, if you would consider yourself my friend also," said Danaïs. "As I am yours."

CHAPTER TWENTY-ONE

LABARQUE had been jailed, but his poison was not yet drawn. His fury at being kept in confinement pending trial—to be held at some undisclosed time when the Judge, the Civil Council, the Plaintiff and the Crown could all be conveniently convened—fed the madness that had already taken hold within him. Night after night the fever in his mind flamed brighter, burning away sleep and pushing him toward a single obsession: revenge.

Disgraced though he was, he still held more than a few men in his grip. He had been a collector of guilty secrets for many years, and he was a master at implicating his partners and hired hands in his own shady actions. It was surprising, he had found, what lengths men would take to protect even the pettiest of their shames.

And he still had his wealth. A whisper into the ear of the shabbiest of the jail workers—a bent, arthritic cleaner who mopped down the hallways and guard room, but not his cell, every night—was all it took to have a note delivered. "What can be the harm of a simple note to a friend?" he had urged. "A note to reassure them in their worry, and beg their remembrance." And he had named a sum to be paid on delivery; a sum that made the credulous simpleton's eyes go round with astonishment and then narrow with greed.

For the day would come, and soon, when LaBarque would be transferred. The building where he was held now was a civil building with many uses, from housing property records to hearing criminal charges. It was not designed to keep long-term prisoners; rather it had a handful of cells for temporary detainment, while the severity of a case was determined. In the years when raiders came, it sometimes held pirates. Most often, the jail block housed only petty thieves or drunken brawlers.

And since his so-called "trial"—LaBarque sneered the word in mockery every time it sounded in his head—would not, apparently, take place for some time, he would undoubtedly be moved to the Regional Prison, far inland from the heavily settled Blanchette coast. That move would provide the opportunity he needed. LaBarque could not claim any ties of friendship, but he could still buy loyalty. Or threaten it.

"Escaped?! For the love of—" Rosalie nearly choked on her own frustration and outrage. "Will we never be free of the man?" Unable to contain herself, she strode to the door and with a cry of anger slammed it shut. Then, feeling foolish at the childish outburst, she opened it again. She closed her eyes and rested her forehead against its cool wooden edge.

Fear. It was fear she felt, in truth. The little display of temper was just her mind's paltry attempt at bravado.

"Don't laugh at me, Tris," she mumbled. She felt his hand on her shoulder, a gentle but insistent pressure that turned her away from the door and into his arms.

"I'm not laughing." Tristan had a buoyant nature, but the messenger's report had erased all good humor. LaBarque's transport had been ambushed on a forest road by armed men, the horses

killed, the guards attacked. Some of the criminals had been appre-
hended, but not before three guards lay dead and LaBarque had
slipped away into the woods.

André spoke up. "If it were anyone else I would expect him to
seek only his freedom—to try to disappear into obscurity, as far
from us as possible. But LaBarque…"

"He's crazy as a coot," concluded Tristan. "Who knows what
he might do? But I agree. This is not about saving his skin. If I
had to, I'd guess he's coming after us."

"You don't think he'll come here?" asked Rosalie. "All the way
to Chênier?"

"I think he'll try," said Tristan. "And Rosie, Dominic had a
good idea. He suggested you come with me to the defense talks
in Gaudette. We can be long gone before LaBarque shows up
here, if he even gets this far. You too, of course," he added, nodding to André.

André shook his head. "I will stay here, if the Queen will extend
her hospitality until his recapture. I am too old to run about
the countryside, and I do not, in any case, believe LaBarque has
much interest in me. But I would be very grateful, and sleep more
soundly, if you would take Rosalie away from here. The sooner,
the better."

"THE SOONER, THE better," said Gabrielle. A real bed, she was
thinking. And a bath and clean clothes and clean hair. She was
tired of roughing it, ready to endure even another bone-jarring
shepherd's wagon if it would get her a comfortable room and a
nurse-maid's help. Gaudette was not far, and Castle Drolet beck-
oned like a very paradise.

Féolan went to speak to the outpost commander, who proved

eager to help his liege-lady. Though there was no carriage on site, he offered them a full-sized cart and horses to pull it, plus horses for Féolan and Derkh to ride. With a mattress laid on the bottom and a good road ahead, Gabrielle could count on a restful journey.

The clop of the horses' hooves made a hypnotic backdrop to Gabrielle's wandering thoughts as the foursome made their way to Gaudette. She lay cradled in the cart, watching a soothing parade of clouds and tree branches. How strange it was to think that this peaceful shaded road was the same route taken just this past spring by the retreating army. Danaïs and Féolan were singing now, clear voices raised in a duet that twined around the beat of hooves and rattle of the cart, the sound so lazy and lighthearted it made the clamor in her memory seem but a dark dream. Yet she knew it had been real: the shouting and confusion, the milling of men and horses, the groans and cries of the wounded and the sudden alarm in her mind that made her turn and struggle against the great tide of men, back to the grim field where her father lay.

Well, that was in the past now. Gabrielle hoped it would stay there, that the defense plan would remain a prudent but untested precaution. One of her brothers would come to Gaudette for the talks, she remembered, anticipating the unexpected reunion with pleasure. With luck she'd be strong enough by then to make the most of his free time. She hoped, with a twinge of apology to Dominic, that it would be Tristan. She wondered if he'd had a chance to see Rosalie yet.

CHAPTER TWENTY-TWO

THE common touch did not come easily to LaBarque. He had disguised many aspects of his personality over the years, but never his rank, unless to aggrandize himself. His mouth drew down in distaste at the touch of these rough clothes, soiled and patched by some common laborer, and he drew his cloak farther over his brow so none would see the disdain glittering in his eye.

It was well for him that he did so, for more showed in his face now than mere contempt for the jostling market crowd. The relentless malice that drove him burned in the dark sockets of his eyes, so that any who marked him shrank from his approach.

He was learning to keep his mouth shut also, for his educated speech betrayed him. In monosyllables he bought a crusty loaf and a slab of pork to lay inside it. It was wholesome enough food, but it disgusted him to eat thus, without plate or service, getting grease on his hands and crumbs down his shirt. No matter. The food, like the clothes, like the anonymity of this stinking crowd of humanity, was only a means to an end. LaBarque retreated to a quieter side street, crouched against a wall and ate mechanically while he planned his next move.

Lots of guards around. Guards at the city gates, questioning peoples' business. Guards here at the market. Word had reached Chênier, then. The castle itself would be shut tight as a drum.

Could he use the same trick twice and enter the castle as he had
the Royal City, hidden in a load of hay? He smelled risk. If rumor
had spread in the city, and he approached the wrong delivery boy,
one unmoved by the coins clinking into his palm...

He would wait and listen and learn how things lay. The Royal
Brat was not one to lie walled up in safety for long. Sooner or
later, the rat would come out of its hole.

BY THE MIDNIGHT bell, LaBarque had visited five different
ale-houses, bought and wasted five mugs of ale and eavesdropped
on untold meaningless conversations. At last he had grown impatient enough to risk a more direct approach. He drained his mug
(the first he had actually drunk) and weaved up to the counter,
acting befuddled.

"Another mug, sir?" The bartender's belly bore witness to many
years of sampling his own goods. It thrust proudly against the
counter as the man came up to serve him.

LaBarque shook his head, spread his hands helplessly. "I must
be in the wrong place. I'm new in town, I was to meet my cousin.
I thought it was here but... He's a groom at the Royal Stables. Is
there a place he'd be likely to..." He left the question dangling.
He knew well enough that pubs tended to have their regular clientele, often groups of men and women who shared a workplace
or a neighborhood. If the royal servants had a regular watering
hole, there was a good chance a hosteller would know of it.

"The Royal Stables, is it? Maybe he was too worn out for
drinkin'. There's been a deal of coming and going at the castle
lately, or so I've heard. But you could try the Queen's Girdle,
just across the road at the corner there. Lot of the castle folk
favor it."

LaBarque flipped a coin onto the counter and pushed out the door.

THE QUEEN'S GIRDLE was, in LaBarque's estimation, "a fetid little armpit." It offered, however, everything the royal servants required of a gathering place: an excellent beer in ample mugs, a congenial host, and best of all, deeply padded red leather benches flanking the back tables—a comfortable and spacious place to rest their bones and exchange gossip. Here they held their own little court, for the inside story on royal goings-on was highly prized and gladly paid for in ale.

LaBarque found a seat not far from the back tables, squeezed in and stared into the beer while his ears did their work. It was not long before he was rewarded for his troubles.

"Oh, aye, she's a lovely girl. Mind you, she has a temper of her own, she does. Didn't she give the Lord Tristan a proper dressing-down just the other day?" This from a clucking, know-it-all voice. It had to be Rosalie under discussion. So the little miss has a shrew's tongue in her head, does she? LaBarque thought. He would soon have cured her of that.

"She didn't!" Braying, delighted shock. That horse-voice could only come from the blowsy redhead he had noticed on the way in. "How could anyone be mad at him, with his lovely smile and all?"

"She was, though. She was all but spittin' fire, let me tell you! Though it weren't long before they was all lovey-dovey again." The two women sighed in apparent satisfaction.

A new voice joined in, a man's.

"I heard there was trouble on the coast and that's why the Martineaus came back here. Is it true the prince was nearly killed?"

"Where've you been, down a hole?" The cluck-hen again. "Of course it's true; everyone knows that old story."

"Ooooh, the treachery of it!" Carrot-top, wallowing in boozy outrage. "Wouldn't I like to get my hands on that one! He'd be missing summat in his britches, if I had my druthers!"

A new voice overrode the chorus of chuckles. "Maybe you'll get your chance, Maude. My brother in the guard says that LaBarque guy gave 'em the slip and might even be headed to Chênier for another try."

The excited shrieks of the women almost drowned out the man's next sentence: "Not that it'll do him any good. Prince Tristan's off to the defense talks already, and the Lady Rosalie with him. Let him come here, I say—make it easier to catch the treasonous devil."

THE HANDS GRIPPING his mug trembled with the effort of self-control. In LaBarque's mind he had hurled it against the wall, crockery shattering, suds frothing down to the floor, and turned on the whole pack of smug, self-satisfied, mindless gossip-mongers like a rabid dog.

Gone. Tristan DesChênes, the man who had become LaBarque's sole reason for being, was gone. The sour taste of defeat rose up in his throat, and he met it with his own seething hatred. He would *not* be sucked down into the muck and mire of failure.

LaBarque's stool clattered to the ground as he jumped to his feet, temporarily stilling the buzz of conversation. He left the stool where it lay and shoved his way through the crowded room. Only a thin thread of will kept him from knifing the first fool who stood in his path. He needed space and air. It wouldn't do to murder someone—the wrong someone—now.

CHAPTER TWENTY-THREE

GABRIELLE sat in a clean, tightly tucked, white bed against clean white pillows, arrayed in a clean white nightgown. Her hair was neatly tied in a Maronnais style: three braids, pulled back and joined into a single thick plait halfway down her back. It had pleased her shy young maid inordinately to be allowed to style Gabrielle's hair so, and she had fussed and labored to make each braid smooth and perfect. In short, Gabrielle was as comfortable and well cared for as could be. And she was bored.

It was a good sign, she knew. Not long ago, she had been too sick and uncomfortable to be bored. Still, she was desperate for something to do: a lap harp to play, or one of the heavy leather-bound books from her father's library to read. Someone to talk to. She craned her neck to catch a glimpse of the view from the window at the foot of her bed. Stretching up straight gave her a warning twinge, but no serious pain. Another good sign.

The king's own bonemender had been charged with her care, and to his eyes Gabrielle's wound appeared to have been a fairly superficial puncture that was healing impressively well, given the rough conditions she had lived in. Still, he had given her every treatment he could think of, seemingly unwilling to believe that nothing more was required than rest and good hygiene. Gabrielle had not revealed how drastic the original injury had been; the

poor man was overawed enough as it was by her rank and reputation as a healer.

A quiet knock—the kind people make when they want to
notify an awake person, but not disturb a sleeping one—made
her brighten. Féolan stuck his head in, smiled to find her so alert
and entered the room. One eyebrow lifted as he took in the total
effect.

"You look…hmm, like some kind of snow spirit. Very neat and
white. I'm afraid to touch you, lest I leave a smudgy fingerprint
on all that white and incur the wrath of your healer—who, by
the way, I believe holds me already in low regard."

Gabrielle laughed. "Why? What's he got against you?"

"I'm not entirely sure. There was a great deal of muttering and
head-shaking just now when I came to see you, all rather cryptic.
He seems to blame me for keeping you out in the bush so long.
I'm sure I heard the phrase 'Should have been seen to sooner.'"

"Oh, I understand." Gabrielle looked to the empty doorway
and lowered her voice to a whisper. "He's upset because there's
nothing left for him to do." She eyed Féolan. "Where did you get
the new clothes? Those aren't Maronnais."

He shook his head. "From Danaïs. He brought extra for the
defense talks. He says he'll come by to see you later today."

"Féolan." Really, she felt very much better. "I'm not worried
about smudges. C'mere."

When he was closer—a lot closer—Gabrielle was taken aback
by the complexity of emotion she could sense. Something was
troubling him. Not wanting to pry, she said nothing. If Féolan
wanted to tell her, he would.

And after a while, he did. With visible resolve, he lifted his head
from where it rested on hers, straightened up and sighed.

"I need to tell you something. And I know what you will say to this," he began. "It is what I would say myself. But I do blame myself for what happened to you." He cut short her protests. "I know. I know you made your own decision to come. I know it was not for me to allow or forbid it. For all I know, you would even make the same decision again." Her emphatic nod confirmed it. "But Gabrielle, sometimes our hearts do not heed our reason. I thought I was going to lose you. And I cursed myself for bringing you into such danger. Can you understand that?"

She hesitated, then nodded. Of course she could understand it. She had blamed herself for her father's death, when no healer on earth could have saved him. Her fingers twined in his. But he wasn't finished.

"So." Féolan ran his free hand through his hair, looked out the window as though to draw strength from the summer air, or maybe escape through it. What could be taxing him so?

"So, you see, now more than ever I do not wish to wrong you again—even if you do not see it as a wrong. And yet I fear I may have done just that."

"Féolan, what are you talking about?" Gabrielle was baffled.

"Gabrielle, my father is concerned that our betrothal vows may have been made—well, rashly." He touched her arm as she bridled. "Please, just listen to the end of this. It's hard enough for me to say."

Féolan's father had been warm and welcoming when they had met. Did he think her an unsuitable match? Inferior, perhaps, with her Human blood. Gabrielle flushed with humiliation. "Gabrielle." Féolan's voice drew her back to him. "He has a point, though I did not wish to hear it at the time. I am the only Elf you have really known. Through me you discovered a kinship of mind—a kinship different from what you have found among Humans."

"Yes, I guess that's true. But Féolan, I'm sorry, I'm not getting the point. That was a wonderful discovery for me. You make it sound like a misfortune." She *was* getting the point, though. She wasn't following the thread that led there, but she could see where it ended. He had doubts about their marriage. Though she flinched away from the pain of that thought, it was unavoidable. His voice went on, and there was no escaping his words, either.

"The thing is this." Another sigh. Like it was his pain, not hers. Gabrielle was glad to feel that flicker of resentment. It strengthened her. "Gabrielle, you haven't had a chance to get to know other Elves. Other male Elves. Perhaps you love me, or believe you love me, simply because I am Elvish. Not because I am truly the best match for your heart. Perhaps, if you had time to live among us for a while, you would find"—another hitch in his breath—"find that another would offer you more."

She had heard words like this before, hadn't she? Oh yes. More than one suitor, when she first came of age, had extricated himself with some variation on the theme of "I am not good enough for you." She had seen through their polite words, known they were just face-saving excuses—and she had played along graciously, for none had captured her heart. But to hear such a thing from Féolan… She couldn't meet his eyes, couldn't stand to see the message she feared they would hold. His voice sounded far away, so loud did the blood pound in her ears, behind her eyes. She had thought she understood this man. Thought they understood each other. Well, she would have the dignity of truth, if nothing else.

"If you no longer wish to marry me," she said, her voice flat and hard with the effort to disguise the hurt, "it would be better to say it outright."

She heard his groan, felt the alarmed tumult of his emotions, but she pulled away from them, too wrapped up with her own.

"Gabrielle, please." The voice soft, pleading. "Feel the truth of what I am about to say to you. You know how to do this. Look as deep into me as you can; you will know if my feelings betray my words." His fingertips brushed her hand, a gossamer touch, gone before she could pull away, the connection there, nonetheless. "Please." His voice broke, and she marveled at the rawness of it. Reluctantly, she raised her eyes and was shocked by the naked need in his face.

"Will you listen?"

Gabrielle was confused again, doubting herself. Everything she had seen of this man—and they had been through much together—spoke of his commitment to her. He deserved a full hearing. She nodded, closed her eyes and tried to still her own turmoil enough to sense his presence. His words dropped directly into her mind.

"There is nothing I have ever wanted as desperately as I want to wed you. And I will love you to my life's end, whether you choose me or no."

And she felt it. Gods of the air, it was impossible not to: it flooded over her warm and bright and golden as the midsummer sun. Love so deep she could drown in it. Desire like hunger. And under all, barely contained fear. Fear of losing her.

Her eyes flew open, wet now with tears. She reached for him, and he wrapped her hands with both of his and pressed his face against them, and she would gladly have carried on from there except she still didn't know what was going on.

"Then what is this about? Féolan, if you do want to marry me then why are you—?"

"It's your happiness I'm worried about, Gabrielle, not mine. I just think if we wait a while, you'll have a chance to live among us and get to know more of us—"

Finally, she understood. And, giddy as she was with relief and that blast of adoration, it struck her as funny.

"How many?"

"What?" Now Féolan was confused.

"How many Elvish men do I have to meet before I am sure?"

"Well it's not really…"

"All of them? Would your father have me meet and assess the merits of all of them, like a cook shopping for mushrooms at the market? Check all the stalls until I find the firmest, whitest, biggest ones?"

"No, of course not, it's just —"

"Twenty then? Three? Féolan, don't you see this is silly? I don't want anyone else. I already love you."

He looked at her, miserable. Tried again. "I don't want to take advantage of you, Gabrielle, just because Fate thrust me in your path. That's all."

She became serious. "Féolan, the very fact that you appeared in my path is part of what makes you right for me. You've walked among Humans. You understand something about their lives. About my life. Because no matter where I live or who I am with, half of me will always be Human."

He smiled. "The impetuous stubborn half. The half that makes you run into the wilderness after lost friends and heal hostile creatures and live like there is no tomorrow."

"Sometimes there *is* no tomorrow, even for Elves," she observed softly. "Féolan, I almost died up there in the mountains. I was so close I was beyond returning. And you called me back. Any Elf, maybe, could have sent his thought after me. But I could only have followed you. Because of the love that is between us. What other proof could I need?"

He was holding her now, so tight it pained her wound but not for anything would she have him stop. Then he laughed.

"I had to force myself to have this conversation, and it was even worse than I feared it would be. And in the end, the only good that came of it all was that I utterly failed!" His fingers traveled along her tight braids.

"Do you know how badly I want to undo these?"

A knock and a liveried servant entered and bowed. "Excuse me, Lady Gabrielle, I didn't know you had a visitor. The king thought you'd want to know: the party from Verdeau has arrived early. Prince Tristan, your brother, is here."

CHAPTER TWENTY-FOUR

"C'MON, it will do us good," Tristan urged. "It will do *me* good, anyway. I've been on my best behavior through four days of talks. The strain is starting to tell."

The two women looked skeptical. Gabrielle had been shaken to hear of the events that had brought Rosalie to Gaudette, but glad of her company over the last few days. By the time the talks had started a few days after their arrival, Gabrielle had been well enough to leave the little clinic (against the Maronnais bonemender's finger-wagging advice) and share Rosalie's room in Castle Drolet. Though so different in personality, they had quickly become fast friends. Now they smirked at each other.

"What?" demanded Tristan, mock-wounded. "What're those faces for?"

"Oh, Tristan, honey," said Rosalie demurely, "it's just, you know, forgive me, but I'm having trouble actually picturing you on good behavior."

"It's true, though," said Féolan. "His conduct was exemplary and contributed greatly to a successful outcome."

"There—you see!" crowed Tristan. "A commendation from the director!" As a distinguished participant who was not directly negotiating, Féolan had been accepted by all as director of the meetings, and Danaïs had been persuaded to stay on and take his place as translator for the Elvish Council. Gabrielle gathered the directorship had been taxing work; Féolan had stopped in on the first evening and collapsed into her chair, proclaiming, "It would be easier to beat them all into silence with the flat of my sword than persuade them to wait their turn!"

"So—how about it? The musicians are said to be the best in the northland. And who knows when we will all be together again?" Tristan looked around the dinner table. There was a hesitant pause.

"Tristan, I'm not sure Gabrielle is up to it," said Féolan.

"Is that what everyone is hemming and hawing about?" said Gabrielle. "I'm fine. I'm almost entirely better and so well rested I'm half-crazy from it. I vote to go!"

"Where's Derkh?" asked Tristan. "He must come too."

"Roaming the city again." Gabrielle had been glad to see Derkh take to the streets of Gaudette—another sign of his growing confidence. "He's been out walking every afternoon. He said he'd be back for dinner, though."

Sure enough, Derkh hurried over and took his place minutes later. "Sorry I'm late," he said. His normally pale cheeks were pink with exertion, his expression eager. "You'll never guess what I just heard."

They all waited while Derkh loaded up his plate with mounds of roast mutton and potatoes.

"Ahh, you make me feel old, Derkh," said Tristan. "I remember when I could eat like that. Now," he said, waving at his only slightly more modest dinner, "I'm past my prime."

Derkh grinned and forked an entire potato into his mouth. Gabrielle was quietly delighted by his bad manners. He had changed. Not long ago such a jest would have made him duck his head in silent embarrassment. Terrible though his experience in the mountains had been, it had somehow done him good.

"So? What did you hear?" prompted Rosalie.

Derkh swallowed painfully, then grabbed for his glass and washed down the huge mouthful with a gulp of wine. "I was down past the market area—there are streets there where the different tradesmen have their workshops and such. And I heard these men talking with an accent—*my* accent! They were Greffaires, I'm sure of it! Right in the streets of Gaudette!"

He sounded positively indignant, Gabrielle thought. Certainly he was baffled at the calm way his news was received.

"Well? Shouldn't we report it or something?" he persisted.

"Um, Derkh, I don't know if you've noticed," observed Tristan, "but you are a Greffaire, and you were in the streets of Gaudette as well. Should we report you?"

"Yeah, but I…" He stopped, wrinkling his forehead in the effort to explain. "You know what I'm doing here. So does King Drolet. But what are *they* doing here?"

"Quite a number of Greffaires have settled in the north of La Maronne, as I understand," remarked Féolan. "We have heard of some near Stonewater, in Loutre and in the sheep country south of Otter Lake. I am not surprised some have come to Gaudette."

Derkh's eyes widened. "You're telling me these are the soldiers who deserted at the invasion? They've settled here, just like that?"

"Not 'just like that,' exactly," corrected Tristan. "I got talking with one of the Maronnais councilors about it over lunch one day. Apparently there was some trouble at first; the Greffaire men hid in the bush and stole from nearby farms to feed themselves. When sheep started to go missing, things nearly got ugly—there was talk of rounding them up."

"Why didn't they?" asked Derkh. Gabrielle understood there was more than curiosity behind the question. His dinner momentarily forgotten, Derkh bristled with intent. His alert posture reminded Gabrielle of a hound straining after a stray scent.

"La Maronne is the most sparsely populated country in the Krylian Basin," explained Tristan, "and spring is a very busy season. A shepherd went after a ewe that had strayed and found her in the hands of a Greffaire 'outlaw.' She was lambing early, and he was attending to her with some skill. The shepherd persuaded the man to come home with him, fed him and put him to work with the shearing and lambing.

"It didn't take long for word to get out that the Greffaires were willing workers, and on the other side that Maronnais farmers had little interest in the politics of war."

"They may have to go farther afield to find work come winter, when things slow down," added Féolan. "But for now, they seem to be faring well enough."

"And now," said Tristan, putting down his own glass with a flourish, "we have news for you."

"You mean more news. I had no idea about those men." Derkh's expression became vague as he contemplated what he had learned. His eyes, gleaming black in the candlelight, snapped back into focus at Tristan's impatient harrumph. "Sorry, what is it?"

"We're going out tonight."

"Out where?" asked Derkh, still not following.

"Out carousing, my lad. Out on the town. Out drinking, to be precise."

CHAPTER TWENTY-FIVE

REVELING in ordinary sights and sounds as only the recently convalesced do, Gabrielle was delighted by every detail of the crowded pub. Crammed around a little table puddled with dribbles of ale, she regarded her companions with blurry fondness. How easily she might never have experienced this moment! Life pulsed through her veins, and the world was good.

The music was as fine as Tristan had promised. The minstrels sang little, but were such masters of their instruments that one did not miss the voices but rather found them in the viol or lute or whistle. Gabrielle was especially entranced with an instrument she had never seen in the south, a Maronnais invention the minstrels called mountain pipes. Its wild lonely wail seemed to her born of the wind that scoured the high empty places.

Tristan, on the other hand, gave all his admiration to the drummer—a hulking bear of a fellow who dwarfed the simple skin drum cradled on his knee. The lap drum, held upright with one hand and played with the other, was a standard instrument throughout the Basin countries, but it had become something entirely new in this player's hands.

"Would you *look* at him!" Tristan was laughing in excited glee. The drummer's arm was a blur as the beater stick traveled the drum, now clacking sharply, now booming out the deep bass of the bottom skin, now skipping a complex rhythm that made them jiggle in their seats. The effect, maybe, should have been over-busy and confusing, but it wasn't: the steady pulse of the rhythm never wavered, and it at once anchored and powered the music.

Danaïs and Féolan were equally rapt, though for different reasons. They came of a people who lived and breathed music, who delighted in the beauty of complex layers of harmony and pure lines of melody. Technical ability did not awe them—Elvish musicians had hundreds of years to perfect their skills. What was new to them was the sheer raw energy of this music, the way it made their hearts jump to the drum or thrill as the viol flew up the scale to its top note. Their own music could be soothing, heart-wrenching, or uplifting. This music was alive.

DERKH ALONE OF the little group was not much of a music lover, but that didn't stop him from enjoying the evening. Truth to tell, he couldn't remember a time when he had felt so happy and relaxed. The revelation about the Greffaire settlers had lifted a last great weight from his mind—the fear that his acceptance in this new land would forever spring solely from the protection of the royal family. Now he saw the possibility of creating his own life here. Perhaps it would be the hard and humble life of a farm hand, but at least he could stand or fall on his own merit.

He craned his neck to look once more around the modest room, taking in the flickering lamps, the great spigotted casks of ale and neat rows of tankards, the men and women with laden trays threading their way among the tables. The cheerful bustle of the place was fascinating.

He hadn't let on, but Derkh had never before been "out carousing." On his fourteenth birthday, his father had taken him to a liquor stop to mark the presentation of his coming-of-age papers, but it had been nothing like this place. The dingy basement room had been dark and silent, dotted with solitary men drinking with such grim determination it seemed to Derkh an ordeal rather than a pleasure. He had earned his father's approval by managing to finish the fiery liquid without coughing, but he had not returned.

As a tune ended, the room erupted into cheers and stamping feet. Derkh let his eyes roam over the crowd: he saw mostly well-dressed men and women, but also people in the coarse plain clothing of laborers, shoulder-to-shoulder with everyone else and served just the same. Except for one frayed old fellow in a mud-spattered cloak, hunched over the bar at the back—he was being given a wide berth. Poor guy, probably smells even worse than he looks, Derkh thought, torn between amusement and pity.

An ear-splitting whistle—thank you, Tristan—brought Derkh's attention back to his friends. He beamed at everyone at once, waggled his tankard in salute and drained it.

IT WAS WELL past midnight, and Gabrielle was flagging. She had seen it in her own patients—a lack of stamina that was the last telltale remnant of illness or injury. Ah well, she hadn't done badly. She leaned her head into Féolan's shoulder, closed her eyes and let her thoughts wander.

They would soon be back in Stonewater. She hoped Nehele had not had her baby early, without her. When they had first become friends last spring, Gabrielle had been excited at the invitation to attend an Elvish birth. Now, though, excitement had turned to concern. Nehele's husband had been slain in the battle against the Greffaires; he would never fasten the baby-stone around his newborn child's neck. The baby would be a comfort to Nehele, but the birth was bound to plunge her into renewed grief as well as joy. Such a labor, Gabrielle knew, could be difficult.

Still thinking like a healer, Gabrielle opened her eyes and let them drift around the table, assessing the state of each of her companions. Tristan was in fine fettle. She knew from experience that he held his ale well, and also that he had the knack of seeming to drink more than he really did. Poor Rosalie, however, had made the mistake of trying to keep up with him. She was propped against Tristan, flushed and disheveled, giggling helplessly at nothing in particular. Gabrielle would be tending her in the morning, without a doubt. Féolan and Danaïs, to her amused surprise, both looked a little bleary. It was subtle—just a settling of the features, a clouding of the usual clear depths of their eyes. Not used to our dark ale, she thought. She might have to remedy that. She had been served a light wine at Stonewater that was exquisite, but she happened to agree with her father's opinion that "There's much to be said for a plain honest ale."

Not that she ever overindulged. It was a discipline ingrained in her along with her bonemender's training, to keep a clear head. "Accidents don't take a holiday just because you do," Marcus had admonished her, and she had seen his words proved true. Gabrielle had stopped refilling her own tankard when the evening was still young.

As, apparently, had Derkh. His dark eyes, when they met hers, were as clear and alert as ever. He lifted his eyebrows at her, mouthed a question: "Okay?" He had noticed her fatigue, then. Gabrielle smiled and nodded, waving away his concern, and pondered the young man's sobriety. Just his natural bent, maybe. Or perhaps he feared losing his head and embarrassing himself. Rosalie will envy you tomorrow, Gabrielle thought.

CHAPTER TWENTY-SIX

THE double doors swung open, a burst of heat and noise spilled onto the street and the cool night air washed over them. Derkh drank it in gratefully; he had not realized how close it had become inside.

"We'll walk you to your rooms," announced Tristan. Danaïs and Derkh had been housed in a comfortable inn not far from the castle, as the king's hospitality was stretched to the limit by official delegates to the talks. "C'mon, Rosie girl, the walk will do you good." Tristan hitched a firm arm about Rosalie, who was distinctly unsteady on her feet, and set a careful pace across the treacherous cobblestone paving. Derkh dropped back a bit from the chattering group to savor the quiet.

As they ambled by, he spied a bundled shape slumped in the gap between two buildings—the same ragged fellow he had seen in the pub, perhaps, or some other homeless beggar. The cloak certainly looked as filthy and ill-used. The man did not stir or raise his head from his bent knees as they passed, and the others, absorbed in talk, took no notice.

Derkh, lost in his own thoughts, soon forgot the unfortunate fellow. He was working on a future Gabrielle had suggested to him back in Verdeau, a future as a skilled craftsman. It had seemed impossible then, but now... Derkh cast his mind over the array of trades he had seen plied in the streets of Gaudette. Would the

Maronnais prove accepting enough to take on a foreigner as a prentice? Or would they keep the Greffaires firmly on the margins, eligible for only the unskilled seasonal work? He couldn't predict. Too much about these people had surprised him already.

The streets were dark and silent, sparsely lit and nearly empty. Derkh's inn was situated away from the busy center of town, chosen by its clientele not for liveliness, but for undisturbed sleep and access to royal doings. Derkh looked ahead at his friends— Gabrielle and Féolan arm in arm, their voices a quiet murmur, Danaïs pacing at their side. Tristan and Rosalie next, Rosie a little steadier now but still walking with the cautious, over-deliberate steps of the unaccustomed drunk. Affection washed through him, and he shook his head, not for the first time, at the unlikely friendships he had made.

How fares my family now? he wondered. Worse than he himself, that was certain. Derkh raised his head to the glittering stars, followed their sweep north, wishing he could send his mother some reassuring message on their wings.

Movement in the corner of Derkh's eye snapped his attention back to earth. A flapping apparition launched itself toward them from a side street, a confusion of dark speed. At first his fuddled eyes thought he was still in the clouds, his star messenger taking ghastly shape before him. Then, as the black figure hurtled into the street ahead of him, the details crystallized into meaning: a shredded black cloak, flying behind a racing man. He caught a flash of teeth, bared in terrible effort. The silver gleam of—

A knife. The nightmare figure brandished a knife as long as Derkh's forearm.

Derkh was airborne before his conscious mind knew what he was doing. Had he not practiced long hours with Col's own

bodyguards against just such a moment? Arms outstretched, head
tucked, he propelled himself forward with all the force his legs
could give him.

And came up just short. Instead of crashing into the assassin's—
for so, surely, was the man's intent?—legs and flinging him to
the ground, Derkh caught a boot in the chin not a breath before
sprawling into the cobblestones himself. Pain jolted through him,
shattering in his right knee, merely brutal everywhere else, but he
had the boot in his grasp and nothing now would loose his grip.
Just as the foot lashed out to kick free, Derkh twisted it, hard,
flipping himself over to get a full rotation. He felt the torque on
the man's knee, heard the grunt of pain, and the cloaked body
hit the ground with a thud.

Derkh's first shocked sight of his opponent's face was paralyzing.
Once down, the man had twisted around and launched himself
on Derkh with the speed of an adder strike. Now Derkh stared
up into an expression so bestial with rage, on eyes so blind with
madness that there seemed nothing human there at all. The man's
full weight was across his chest, his knife raised high, and all Derkh
could do was stare, sickened, understanding that he had become
the assassin's victim.

MOVE, BOY! Col's voice boomed, and Derkh was back in the
grappling ring. Greffaire soldiers faced combat in armor, but Col
had insisted Derkh also learn hand-to-hand fighting from the best
trainers in the country—as much for protection against fellow
soldiers who might find a scrawny adolescent an easy target, as
against hypothetical enemies of the state.

His left leg whipped up, and with that move he understood that
his assailant had more conviction than technique. Not only were
his legs unpinned, but the dramatically raised blade gave him an

obvious opening. Hooking his leg up and around the man's raised arm to block the knife thrust, he also managed to rock the heavy body back enough to free his left arm.

Derkh groped for the knife sheath at his waist, found it, and had his own blade sunk into the assassin's neck in one swift upward thrust. With a gurgling cry, the man fell heavily against him, his long blade ringing against the stone beside Derkh's ear. Gods, where are the others? he wondered wildly, not realizing they had barely had time to be aware of his struggle before it was over. They were at his side even now, though he could not see them. His senses were blotted out by the dying body pressed against him. Hot blood flooded over his face and glued clingy webs of hair against his cheeks and eyes; the stench of filth wrapped about him like a poisonous cloud.

As the sickening weight was dragged off him, Derkh rolled to his hands and knees and vomited onto the blood-slick stones.

IT WAS FÉOLAN and Danaïs who pulled LaBarque off of Derkh.

Gabrielle waited in an agony of impatience, desperate to get to him. Then, just as she reached out to him, he shuddered and lurched up onto his knees. She understood then that Derkh was all right. No mortally wounded man cares where his vomit lands.

Though she longed to stay and comfort him, she forced herself to follow the bonemender's protocol: the greatest need first. She turned to the cloaked figure, now lying spread-eagled some distance from Derkh. A terrible scarecrow, his features frozen in a snarl of hatred. Gabrielle swallowed, fighting her own revulsion. She forced herself to approach, to kneel beside him, to check for pulse and breath. There was none.

Backing away in guilty relief, she turned and looked for someone to tell. Tristan was occupied with Rosalie, who was sobbing uncontrollably. She caught the words, "It's over now, Rosie. Finished for good, now," and finally grasped what had happened. She tried to match the ruin that lay before her with the rich merchant Tristan had described and could not. He had been burned away, consumed by his own malice.

Féolan and Danaïs were with Derkh. They had steered him to a clean patch of road, wiped his face and hands and wrapped him in Féolan's cloak. Now all three looked a question at her. She shook her head. "He's dead," she said.

Derkh flinched at the words, his shoulders hunching as though against a blow. Gabrielle was pierced with pity for him, pity and anger too at the injustice of it, that one boy should have to suffer such a relentless string of terrors. Her eyes prickled and then swam with tears as she made her way to him.

"HE'S DEAD."

Gabrielle's eyes filled with tears. She walked toward him, her face stricken, and if Derkh could have cast himself into the black pit of his own misery and disappeared, he would have done so.

What have you done? he accused himself. He could barely remember what had triggered the incident. You tackled some crazy old bugger who maybe didn't even know you were there, terrified him into fighting for his life and killed him. All his good resolve had come to nothing. He had hurt her again. It was hard to imagine how one could repay a healer's kindness more cruelly than with a corpse.

He couldn't face her.

Nevertheless she stood in front of him, bent before him,

searched for and found his blood-sticky hands, grasped them and pulled him gently to his feet. And because he was beholden to her, because he deserved whatever she wished to say to him, he met her eyes when she spoke his name.

To his confused astonishment what he saw there was not disgust or anger at all. She was smiling through her tears, and her hands cupped his face the way the *seskeesh* had when they said farewell.

"You saved him, Derkh. You saved my brother's life. If you hadn't... If he had..." Sobs overtook her, and oblivious to the bloody mess down his front, she wrapped her arms around his neck and pulled him against her.

Derkh held her waist gingerly. Too much had happened, too fast; he seemed to have missed something important.

Click, click. Pictures flared into focus in his head, like the tumbles falling into place in a lock: the ragged old man at the pub, the derelict slumped over in the street. It was him. He followed us.

Click. Rosalie—Rosalie who by all accounts knew how to keep her head in a crisis—crying like a terrified child in Tristan's arms.

Click. LaBarque, escaped from his guards far to the south.

He knew now who he had killed. His instincts had been right, after all. Tears of relief welled up in his own eyes. He closed them, tightened his grip on the best friend he had ever had and thanked every supernatural being he could think of that this time he had managed to avert, not cause, disaster.

CHAPTER TWENTY-SEVEN

I T felt strange to be heading north, back to Stonewater, rather than south with Tristan. The paths of their lives were drawing apart; this time next year Tristan and Gabrielle would be living at opposite ends of the Krylian Basin. He'd be happy on the Blanchette Coast, Gabrielle was sure, as she would be happy with Féolan. But she would miss him, and Rosalie too.

"You're still coming to Chênier for the winter?"

The Verdeau delegation waited a respectful distance down the road, while Tristan and Rosalie made their farewells to the others. Gabrielle, Féolan, Derkh and Danaïs had ridden with them to the south gate. They were all traveling on horseback this time, courtesy of King Drolet. Gabrielle smiled at Tristan. "Yes. Tell Mother I'll be there by…" She cocked her head at Féolan, considering. "When, do you think? I'd like to arrive in time to help with the Winter's Eve planning."

"Beginning of Twelvemonth, at the latest, then?" suggested Féolan.

Tristan nodded in satisfaction. "Good. And then Gabrielle and I will while away the winter snows planning our weddings without you two!"

"We shall have to be married twice, then," said Rosalie tartly, "for I shall be doing the same in Blanchette!"

Tristan leaned far out on his saddle and planted a last kiss on his sister's cheek.

"Gotta go. Hey, and think about my idea—the double wedding. We could throw the most fantastic party in the history of Verdeau!"

Gabrielle's smile followed Tristan and Rosalie down the road. She actually liked the idea of a ceremony that would celebrate the bond with her family as well as her new life with Féolan. She had a funny feeling, though, that Elves might not consider "a most fantastic party" the primary function of a wedding. A convincing demonstration of my maturity for Féolan's father, she thought, and then gave herself a mental shake. Féolan had assured her Shéovar's reservations had nothing to do with her personal qualities, and she intended to take him at his word.

Gabrielle turned the big bay horse back to her own companions, wishing it were Cloud she was riding. As soon as they were through town and nicely underway, she would put her mind to getting to know this one. It bothered her now to pull on a horse's mouth.

"HOW BIG A town is Loutre?" Derkh shaded his eyes and peered down the road, as if better eyesight might give him a glimpse of the place.

They were leaving the main road about ten miles south of Loutre, taking a narrow, overgrown trail that skirted the nearly uninhabited north shore of Otter Lake.

"Not very," answered Féolan. "Less than half the size of Gaudette, I would guess. But it's surprisingly busy—it's the only substantial town in the north reaches, so a lot of trade and traffic goes through it." Derkh did not reply, just nodded as he guided his horse into the turnoff.

They stopped to eat and rest in the early afternoon, at a place where great slabs of flat rock, warmed by the noon sun, thrust out into the water. Gabrielle stretched out on a finger of stone that allowed her to trail both hands in the clear lake, tucked her rolled-up cloak under her cheek and closed her eyes.

She looked too comfortable to disturb, so Féolan pulled off his boots and dangled his feet over a wide ledge of his own. Cool water lapped at his ankles. Soon, another pair of feet joined his—very pale feet that looked to have rarely seen the light of day. He watched Derkh's toes curl up at the first cold shock, then relax and float in the lake.

"You want to let those feet out into the sunlight more often," he joked. "They look like big aquatic mushrooms."

"I've never done this before," Derkh replied softly, and that seemed to Féolan as sad as anything he had yet learned about Derkh's life. There was a pause, while they both watched the strange wavery shapes of their feet, and then Derkh spoke again, serious and a little hesitant.

"There's something I want to ask you, but I don't wish to be a burden. If what I ask is too much, I want you to tell me so freely."

Féolan turned and searched the boy's face. Derkh was clearly nervous, but returned Féolan's gaze with steady eyes. A boy no longer, Féolan corrected himself.

"Ask me," he said simply.

"You told me that while you were in Greffier you posed as a smith, so that must mean you know how to do it?"

Féolan gave a brief laugh, remembering how near he had come to disaster over a simple piece of horse harness. "I know the basics. But I am better at jewelry than useful metal work."

"Oh." Derkh seemed disappointed. "Well, that would still be better than nothing. I was wondering if you might teach me."

"Teach you smithing?" Féolan looked at Derkh in surprise. Derkh colored, the old self-consciousness rising, but kept his head high.

"I've been thinking about a trade, so I could earn my keep here. I was watching the men in Gaudette, the tradesmen, and I kept coming back to the smiths. I thought if you could teach me so I had at least some skill, I might find a smith who would take me on as a prentice, even though I'm…" He shrugged.

You're scrawny for a smithy. The words came back to Féolan before he realized Derkh had been talking about his nationality, not his size. Still, it was a problem. Féolan was over six feet tall and broad-shouldered, but the Greffaire soldier who said that to him had been right—he *was* scrawny for a smithy. He pulled his thoughts together.

"Derkh, I would be happy to teach you what I know. Better still, if you like it I will introduce you to our head smith and you can learn properly from him."

Derkh's relieved grateful smile made it harder to say his next words.

"But…I have to wonder if it is the right trade for you. Smithing is heavy work. Most full-time blacksmiths are big powerful men, especially in the back and arms." He stopped. Derkh's smile had broadened into a wide grin.

"You think I'm too small."

"Well, it's just—"

"I don't think you need to worry about that. I don't expect to be small much longer."

The confidence in Derkh's voice was striking. Féolan raised an inquiring eyebrow.

"You remember how my father was built?" Derkh asked.

He remembered. Commander Col had reminded him of a bull—all neck and shoulders.

"He had four brothers. They all look like that. And they all got their growth late. I may not end up tall, but I expect I'll have muscle enough for the job."

Féolan took a more careful, appraising look at the slim young man beside him. This time he sought out the underlying frame and noticed for the first time the square stretch of Derkh's shoulders, the sturdy girth of his wrist, the big hands. Like a rawboned colt, he thought.

"I guess you have chosen well, after all," he said.

IT WAS BORING up on the wall. Matthieu had been so excited when he managed to scale it, and for a long time the view from on high, combined with the smug knowledge that Madeleine didn't know where he was, kept him interested. Whenever anyone came out of the castle into the front courtyard, he scooted along the broad rock to the place where the great spruce tree swept its branches over the edge and hid in the scratchy boughs.

But no one had come out for ages now. As five bells rang out, only determination kept him from climbing down and finding something more fun to do. Determination, and the growing suspicion that he might not know how to get down.

It didn't matter. He was the lookout, and the messenger had said Uncle Tristan and Rosie would be back late today, and he was going to see them first. Before Yves, before anybody. And when they came, Uncle Tristan would get him down.

He checked the road again. Nothing. Nothing, nothing, nothing.

Matthieu blew out air in frustration, like he'd seen his mama do. He straddled the wide wall and peered over the edge. It was a long way down. He was afraid to hang his legs over and try to find footholds he couldn't see. What if he couldn't hold on?

Where were they? He checked again—and this time, as he watched, a group of figures on horseback rounded the bend. Even from this distance he could make out Tristan, and Rosie, and the general and a bunch of others.

Vindicated, proud of his boundless patience, Matthieu watched the small figures gradually get bigger. Most of them split off and followed the road into town. Two made for the gatehouse.

A new, and even better, idea came to him. If he could sneak right up onto the gatehouse roof… He scooted along, being really, really careful because if Yves noticed him he'd catch it for sure.

He wasn't bored anymore.

Tristan rode through the gate with a flourish, saluting Yves and reining in his horse sideways to bow Rosie through. As he bent low over his horse's neck, he addressed her in a whiny, nasal voice distinctly reminiscent of a certain Verdeau councilor.

"Welcome, most illustrious guest, to Castle DesChênes, home to the most valiant and attractive bachelor prince in all of—" He ducked as Rosalie tried to swat him with her reins.

A dark shape plummeted onto his back, pinning him against his horse and clutching his neck. Tristan's heart leapt into a panicked gallop. It can't be, he thought wildly. Even in death, he stretches after me! He grappled for the hands choking him, yanked them away. Heard a sound that finally penetrated the clanging alarm in his head.

Giggling.

He looked up. Rosalie was bent over the saddle, laughing so

hard the tears streamed from her eyes. Yves had turned away and
covered his mouth with a gnarled hand, but he couldn't hide his
shaking shoulders. Tristan felt the hands he had prised from his
neck. Very small hands, they were. Very small.

"Matthieu!" He reached back, grabbed the small body and
swung it in front of him. Big brown eyes looked up at him, unsure,
it seemed, whether to laugh or cry. He held the little boy close
against his heaving chest. "Eternal night, Matthieu, you nearly
scared the life out of me!" He stroked the small back while his
breathing steadied. Spoke gently: "Did I hurt you?"

Matthieu shook his head no against him. "But I never heard
you scream like that before. It was—"

"Very valiant," said Rosalie.

A hoot of laughter escaped from behind Yves' hand.

GABRIELLE WRAPPED HER hands carefully around the slippery
squirmy bundle of life as it slid from Nehele's body. A boy, warm
and strong and turning pink already with his first breaths. She
eased him up to his mother's waiting arms, tucking a soft blanket
warm from the fire round them both.

Nehele cradled the tiny, perfect body between her breasts,
weeping and laughing at once. Every woman in the room—
Nehele's mother, her sister and Gabrielle herself—became teary
at the sight.

Gabrielle watched quietly while Nehele stroked her baby's
hair and cheek, gazed into his eyes, murmured and sang to him.
Every single baby she had ever seen born had seemed to her the
loveliest creature ever made. Every one, it seemed, had eyes full
of mystery and wonder. But never had she seen a babe with eyes
like this one—eyes like new violets glowing with dew, eyes even

in their first minutes seeming to hold endless depths. She tried to be attentive to her work, to watch the baby's breathing and color, to monitor Nehele's recovery, but she kept losing herself in those mesmerizing new eyes.

Nehele's mother brought her a cup of tea, squeezed her shoulder in wordless thanks before returning to her daughter's side.

This is what I was meant to do, thought Gabrielle. Not wield a bow or make war plans or even stitch together chopped-up soldiers. Just the ordinary work of a healer.

She sat back, basking in the peaceful reverence she always felt after a healthy birth. Later tonight she would leave Nehele in the care of her family and walk back along Stonewater's winding paths, under the great orange autumn moon. Féolan would be waiting for her.

Their future lay ahead, a promise that had yet to take shape. But life was not lived in the future. Life was right now, right here, in her hands.

She examined the cup she held—the gloss of it, the rich color, the exquisite transparency of the liquid within—and drank deep.

Holly Bennett is the Editor-in-Chief of Special Editions at *Today's Parent* magazine, where she has worked for nineteen years. Her first novel, *The Bonemender*, was named an International Reading Association Children's Book Award Notable and a New York Public Library Book for the Teen Age. She's glad to have found a more respectable outlet for her love of fantasy than beating her children at *Star Wars Trivial Pursuit*. Holly lives with her family in Peterborough, Ontario.